I0638607

THE VEILED LAGOON

An Adam Fraley Mystery

by

Henry Hoffman

Martin Sisters Publishing

Published by

Martin Sisters Publishing, LLC

www. martinsisterspublishing. com

Copyright © 2013 Henry Hoffman

Martin Sisters Publishing, LLC, Kentucky.
ISBN: 978-1-62553-052-3
Literary Fiction
Mystery/Suspense
Printed in the United States of America
Martin Sisters Publishing, LLC

~ To Marlene and Jim

Acknowledgements

My gratitude to Barbara Beattie for her assistance in the preparation of the manuscript.

I would thou wert either cold or hot. If you are lukewarm, I shall spew you out.
--Revelation 3:15

CHAPTER ONE

For Vickie Murin to have vowed never to drive again after dark represented a significant change of mind. Like many of the younger generation, she considered it an old person's worry. So she believed until the night of her last birthday when she emerged as the sole survivor of a trail of carnage left by a drunk driver. Yet, here she was a scant year later, headed home in the dead of night along a deserted rural road as worn as the pickup truck she was driving. She could thank her husband for that--- for the vehicle as well as the shortcut advice.

She pressed on the car radio for some company.

Tens of thousands of demonstrators, mostly young, stormed the Berlin Wall today to hack away at the stark symbol of Soviet oppression. It was the latest act in the disintegration of the communist empire as freedom continued to extend across the Soviet Union bloc.

Not the only thing disintegrating she whispered below the announcer, as she punched the radio off in frustration. No sooner had the stark awareness of her isolated circumstance crossed her mind again than she realized she was no longer alone. In her rearview she spotted a vehicle with blue and red flasher lights closing fast in the dark. She glanced at the speedometer. What was she doing wrong? She was well within the limit.

She eased her car onto the gravel shoulder of the road, recalling the warning her husband once voiced to her, about fake cops pulling young women over for nefarious reasons.

A moment later she heard the crunch of gravel as the unmarked vehicle pulled in behind her. Immediately, the driver doused his lights, heightening her concern. Is this standard procedure?

For a moment, nothing stirred except for her brain cells, which were processing at near panic speed. She probed her purse, first for her driver's license then her pepper spray. Seconds later a figure stepped out of the shadows and stooped to peer into the driver's window. A single glance immediately sent her forefinger flying to the control button. She pressed it down with enough force to break a nail. "Alex, you nearly scared me to death!" she snapped. "What are you doing out here?"

He leaned his frame halfway into the window. "I need to see you," he said with great deliberation before turning to circle the pickup, entering on the passenger side.

"Careful, you are going to sit on a pumpkin-cheesecake pie I brought you from the party," she said, scooting it from his path. "It has bourbon in it...your favorite kind," she added with a smile. "Aren't you the one who's always saying how it's something to die for?"

She watched intently a wan smile form on his face, as he extended a hand to the back of her head, gently kneading her hair in the first gesture of affection she could recall from him in some time. Now might be a good time to bring up the matter of a new car to replace the pickup, she thought.

He reached over with his free hand to turn off the vehicle's lights. Something was on his mind...the same thing that'd been lingering on it for months now, she presumed.

She narrowed her eyes. "What are you doing out here?" she repeated in a low, inquisitive tone. "I thought you were on special assignment over in Tampa Palms."

8

"There was a change of plans," he said in his matter of fact way, leaving it at that.

She knew better than to press him on it. It's a departmental matter, he likely would say, as though she had no relationship whatsoever with the department.

His hand continued to knead the back of her head when unexpectedly she felt his fingers tighten into a grip, leaving her no time to react, much less comprehend, as he drove her head full force into the steering wheel, a blow that sent a shudder through the dashboard.

•••

After a brief pause to check on traffic, he pulled her head back from the wheel and checked for signs of life while maintaining a firm grip. Detecting a weak pulse and faint breath, he carefully examined the contusion on her forehead, calculating the angle and distance between it and the steering wheel. Once again, he rammed her head, striking it in the identical spot as before, knocking the remaining life out of her.

He released his grip, allowing the lifeless form to slump in the seat. He checked to make sure there were no marks on the back of her neck. As expected, her hair served as a cushion, ensuring there were none.

He again looked for traffic. Observing none, he unfastened her seatbelt and exchanged places with the body, shifting it enough to allow him to slip into the driver's position, all the while careful to avoid the pie and the blood streaming from her head.

He switched on the vehicle's headlights, ignited the engine, and entered the highway.

Several hundred yards ahead stood a small canal bridge. Fifty yards or so short of the span the road veered sharply to the left. On reaching the curve, however, he kept the pickup on a straight path, steering the vehicle off the road and on a direct line toward a steep embankment. He tapped the brakes ever so slightly to bring the vehicle to a soft stop ten yards from the canal. Setting the hand brake, he opened the door and hurriedly shifted her body back behind the wheel. One last time he checked the interior of the vehicle, making sure he left nothing behind he would later regret. He then released the brake and gave the truck a shove forward, closing the door as he did so. He watched as it gathered speed down the incline and descended over the bank, sticking head first in the shallow water, its taillights still blazing from its exposed rear.

Turning his attention from the taillights to the ground, he checked for footprints. Fortunately, a cover of dried pine needles came to his assistance, concealing his tracks.

As a precaution he made sure he stepped softly as he made his way back to the squad car. Handprints, he needn't worry about. It was the family vehicle after all.

He traveled parallel to the road on the way back, several times stumbling over small crevices and mounds of dirt in his haste. The scented night air hung still and heavy over the scene, the quiet broken by the chirps and trills of insects backed by a chorus of cicadas. Far away, streaks of lightning chased one another across the horizon followed moments later by muted rolls of thunder, as a line of thunderstorms moved off Tampa Bay and into the gulf. A mixture of pine and cypress trees bordering the road provided him cover from highway traffic, until he spotted his vehicle through their silhouetted figures. In the time it took to reach the car, only two motorists had passed, both traveling at a high rate of speed. Entering the car he debated whether to return the way he came or continue on in the direction of the bridge. It wouldn't hurt to take a look at the scene, he decided. First, though, he took out a pocketknife, sliced a sample piece of the pumpkin-cheesecake pie he had carried back to the car and sank his teeth into it, savoring every bite. His wife…his ex-wife…was right. The touch of bourbon was there for the tasting.

Finishing off his snack, he paused a moment to let a lone truck rumble by, before easing his car back onto the road. Crossing the bridge he was able to see clearly the beams from the taillights of the half-submerged vehicle off to his right, something the two drivers who had passed in the interim apparently had failed to notice. Nonetheless, someone soon would and in the end it would be to his benefit.

Two hours later he was cruising the streets of Tampa Palm when he received a call on the car radio.

"Detective Murin---calling Detective Murin."

He recognized the heavy voice, tipping him to what was coming.

"Murin here."

"Detective Murin---Sheriff Cartwright. I think you had better return to the station. It's about your wife Vickie..."

CHAPTER TWO

Charlton Quigley had a priestly face, the kind you don't associate with an ex-marine. It was Adam Fraley's first impression of the elderly man sitting across the desk from him with the Semper Fi insignia sewn into his khaki shirt pocket.

"You say you got wind of this place from the back of your church bulletin?"

"Yes, sir, Mr. Fraley" the man replied in a voice hoarsened by age.

Adam recalled a nearby shop owner once boasting some of his best clients came via such an ad. Best bang for the smallest buck, the neighbor had said, prompting Adam to place one in a couple of local church publications. "What can I do for you?" he asked, giving himself some of the credit for the chance connection between the priestly face and the church bulletin.

"Well, I should say right off this might not be the proper approach to take to my problem, but I thought I would give it a try," the man said, scooting a piece of lint from his shirt collar.

"And your problem?" Adam asked.

Quigley folded his arms and exhaled deeply, his soldier shoulders showing some sag in their battle against time.

"About a year ago I started patronizing this corner coffee shop down the street from the complex I live in. It's an early morning habit of mine. I go alone and sit and think, mostly about little things, occasionally about a big one..."

Here's hoping he gets to the big one fast, Adam thought. He had a criminal justice class to make.

"...I'm a widower, with no children and no close relatives," the man continued, paring down the profile. "I live in a retirement community where everybody pretty much keeps to themselves, which is fine by me. To give you an idea of how things are there, a sign was passed out to everyone in the complex to hang on their door. One side says "awake," the other side says "asleep." You'd think a 'Do Not Disturb' would suffice. Anyway, that's the world I live in--- there and the corner coffee shop. An old soldier dutifully fading away, just like General McArthur famously spoke. I say this because my entire life soon changed because of one young woman who interrupted my fading away. She was a young lady who worked at the corner shop."

Quigley paused as if reluctant to continue.

"And?" Adam asked, nudging him along.

"One morning, during her break, she came over to join me at my table. I was taken aback...pleasantly so. Here's an old regular who comes in almost every day---sits alone and dreams away the rest of his days over coffee. The next thing I know, I look up and there's a fairly attractive young lady across the table engaging me in conversation."

"Some guys have all the luck," Adam responded, humoring the old fellow.

"Yes, I always wanted a daughter, except this was more like a grandfather thing, considering the age difference."

"Too bad there are young women running around with neither," Adam offered, wondering at the same time where this was headed.

"Told her that part about always wanting a daughter," Quigley said, unfolding his arms and clasping his hands against a stomach as flat as the backside of the chair he was occupying. "Not right away of course, only after we got to know each other a bit."

Quigley threw his hands out. "Well, whatever her motivation, the next thing you know, it turned into a daily ritual...a regular morning coffee klatch between the two of us."

14

"Sounds as though she brought a little joy into your life," Adam said.

Quigley eyed him as if through a rifle sight. "Brought is the right word, since she is now dead."

"Oh, yeah?" Adam responded. He was about to learn where this was headed. "Sudden, I take it."

"Single car accident...around midnight."

"Cause?"

Quigley refolded his arms. "According to the newspaper accounts and the staff at the coffee shop, she fell asleep at the wheel."

Adam nodded and awaited the there's-more-to-the-story part written all over his face.

"I suppose you are wondering why I am bringing this to you."

He again nodded.

"Her name was Vickie," he said with a hint of emotion. "She and I didn't speak much of deeply personal matters---mostly superficial stuff---small talk."

An ex-marine with a priestly face who enjoys kindly small talk, and he made it through the rigors of boot camp and a career, no less.

"What I did learn from her is that she had this deep-seated fear of driving after dark. It had to do with an accident she was in a year ago in which her best friend was killed." Quigley shook his head "She was the sole survivor."

"Her fault?" Adam asked.

"No. Her friend was driving. They were blindsided by a drunk driver."

"So, what is it you're looking for?"

"I'm looking for a second opinion. I read the newspaper account of what the accident investigators had to say. Now I'm seeking your opinion."

"You're suspicious?"

Quigley stared straight at him. "One hard lesson I learned in the service is that official investigations are only as truthful as

15

the people who conduct them. I do not know any of the officials who conducted the investigation into Vickie's death. But I do know you, Mr. Fraley, if only on the barest level. Somehow I feel obligated to get a second opinion for nothing more than a selfish reason...to close the book on my life. I don't mean to play the sympathy card, but I was diagnosed with the big C a while back. There's this new thing called the PSA test. It says my cancer is in a late stage. Not that it matters. I have outlived both family and friends." He paused to chuckle at the thought to come, his shoulders quaking up and down. "And now I have no one to scatter my ashes," he said. "In all seriousness I hate seeing a young person's life snuffed out before they have the opportunity to experience the fullness of it. Vickie often spoke of having children someday...living out the family life for the remainder of her days, which turned out to be a pipe dream."

"Did she give you any reason or indication that would leave you suspicious of the circumstances surrounding her death?"

"Nothing substantial. Not long ago I commended her for having a lot of good traits. Her response was 'apparently not enough to be a good wife.' I was taken aback a little by her comment but did not pursue it."

"She was married?"

"Yes."

"Her last name?"

"Funny thing is, I came to learn her last name through the newspaper report. We were on a first name basis only. But to answer your question...her last name was Murin."

"And there were no kids."

"No. Her husband was all Vickie had. As I mentioned, her best friend was killed in a previous auto accident, and like me, she was an only child. Both of her parents died young. Maybe that's why she catered to me."

"What does the husband do for a living---the widower, that is?"

"He's a detective for the sheriff's department."

•••

Adam glanced at the calendar and the clock. He still had plenty of time for a quick trip to the public library to look up the article on the Vickie Murin accident before his scheduled interview with a prospective assistant.

Ten minutes of scrolling through two reels of microfilm landed him on the article entered halfway down the front page of the local news section.

Woman killed in single-car accident.

A 22-year old woman died in a one-car accident on a truckers' road in rural Hillsborough County late Thursday night. According to accident investigators, the woman's car veered off the road and landed in a canal a short distance from the roadway. There were no witnesses to the accident on the lightly traveled route. The victim was identified as Vickie Murin of Tampa. Investigators said the woman was returning home from the Starlight Dinner Theater where she was appearing in a play. Officials stated the driver was wearing no seatbelt at the time of the accident and died from a massive head injury. They also said there was no indication the victim was driving under the influence of alcohol or drugs. Investigators said it is likely the driver fell asleep at the wheel.

A few more twists of the reel brought him to a death notice.

Vickie Murin, 22, of Tampa, FL died on Tuesday, November 9th, 1989. She is survived by her husband, Alex Murin. Arrangements by Hogan Funeral Home.

Not much to latch onto, he concluded, though his expectation level was low to begin with. He scrolled through several more issues of the paper but was unable to locate an obituary.

Shutting down his search, he made a mental note…make visit to Starlight Dinner Theater.

On his return to the office, he made a side-trip to a highway patrol station to retrieve a copy of the official accident report.

Back at his desk, he rapidly scanned its contents while keeping an eye out for his applicant's arrival.

As accident reports go, it was standard fare, starting with the date, time and place of the incident, followed by the details…a

17

description of the driver, the vehicle, the weather, the property damage, and ending with a diagram of the scene. Also entered was a list of the contents of the truck, including items in the victim's purse and in the glove compartment.

Through his window Adam spotted his applicant heading toward the office. He set the report aside, wondering if the old warrior's suspicions were little more than bitter conjecture.

•••

"Combat duties?" the young woman sitting across the desk from him asked in disbelief.

"They're what my former boss defined as 'other' duties, Ms. Fugit," Adam said. "In addition to the office manager responsibilities, I may have to call on you for occasional field work. Fraley Investigations is a small undertaking and still in its infant stage. It formerly was known as Peterson Investigations until my old boss Pete Peterson decided to retire to the Keys. I took on the operation when he left." He gestured to the spare surroundings, "and in a small office, as you may well know, you often end up performing duties outside your normal range."

"Like what?" she asked.

"Minor surveillance. Tailing a cheating spouse---sitting in on a stakeout---assignments along those lines. Many people feel it adds excitement to the job."

"It would be particularly exciting in my case," the woman replied, "since I have no experience in those sorts of things."

"In this business you learn by doing. The private investigation trade is in a transition stage," Adam explained. "We've tossed out the binoculars and replaced them with the computer. We've gone from the outside to the inside, which is why I need an experienced office manager with computer skills on board

"Listen, Tamara---mind if I call you Tamara?"

"I prefer Tamra."

"Listen, Tamra---when people apply for a position in a detective agency, there's usually a thrill-seeking component stoking their interest in the job. It comes from watching too much crime fiction on television. The point to remember is you have the right of veto power when it comes to the 'other' duties."

"As your former boss might ask---is there combat pay for the combat duty?"

He already had been sold on her earlier in the interview. In addition to her experience in office skills, she exhibited the bright, steely demeanor one might find in a woman sitting behind a library reference desk. Behind her stylish rimless glasses beamed discerning green eyes framed by dark red hair rolled to the back. Yes, her moxie level was yet to be determined, the red hair notwithstanding. The nuts and bolts of the business he could teach. Moxie, he could not.

"Time and a half for combat pay," he said.

He awaited a response but none followed.

"I do have one final question for you, a hypothetical one," Adam said. "Suppose you were walking alone across a large vacant field and you came across a paper bag stuffed with nothing but unmarked twenty and fifty dollar bills totaling several thousand dollars. What would you do with it, if anything?"

"I'd find out whom it belonged to," she answered with no hesitation.

Adam locked eyes with the applicant. "And...?"

She gave a slight shrug of the shoulders. "That's my answer."

Adam continued. "This is the office manager's desk," he said, patting its top. "Mine is over there," he added, pointing past a small cluster of red leather lounge chairs and planters sprouting ficus trees to a companion desk at the opposite end of the cramped room. "As I said, you'll learn on the fly. The biggest part of the job is determining what is fact or fiction. Often it turns out to be simple miscommunication. We are a licensed agency and very selective in our choice of clients, though the cases cover a wide range of human behavior...or misbehavior, I should say. Basically, we gather information and

19

let the client, or in some instances law enforcement agencies, make the decision as to what to do with it. We decide whether to accept a client's request on a case-by-case basis. The final decision is mine. You will be responsible for the initial screenings. There are written guidelines I will give you to help in the selection process. "

Adam leaned back in his chair and folded his hands in his lap. "Any questions?"

"Yes. I have two," she said. "Without revealing any trade secrets, can you tell me why you were expecting more to my sack-of-cash response?"

Adam shrugged. "Sure. I was baiting you, but to your credit, you didn't bite. The answers applicants give usually run the gamut...'I'd turn it over to authorities,' many say, thinking it's the answer the interviewer wants to hear...'I'd keep it all,' a few dare say. Some of the others...'I'd keep a portion of it and turn in the rest'...'I'd hold on to it till I heard if there's a reward in the offing'...'I'd leave it be for fear I would become involved in illegal activity' and so on. And then there's the detective's answer...the one you gave. Everything else follows. Second question?"

She glanced around the room. "Did you do the décor for this office?" she asked, without cracking a smile.

"My former boss is responsible. He wanted a Florida motif. I did manage to talk him out of the exotic bird."

"Are you going to perform a background check on me?" she asked in half jest.

"Should I?" Adam asked in return.

"Not unless you want to catch up on some sleep," she said with a glitter in her eyes.

Adam smiled. "I've already done the background check. Anything else you'd like to know?" he asked.

"When do you expect to complete the interviews?' she asked.

"They are completed. The job is yours, if you're willing to accept it."

She gave a final glance around the office in the same manner a woman would eye a bachelor's pad on first entering. She then nodded a yes, as if to say why not give it a shot.

CHAPTER THREE

The Starlight Dinner Theater, located east of town, provided middlebrow cultural entertainment for those suburbanites averse to making the long trek to the center city for their night out. The Starlight's distinguishing component, often upstaging the stage production, was its retractable glass roof, a feature that made memorable Adam's sole visit to the theater several years earlier when the roof stuck during a surprise thunderstorm, leaving half the guests, including Adam and his companion, scrambling for cover. What made the episode fitting was the scheduled fare for the evening---the theatrical version of Singing in the Rain. This time around Adam was playing the role of insurance adjuster, seeking a replay of the scene preceding the final one in Vickie Murin's life.

"Rose Garland, the stage manager, would be the person to speak to," a box office clerk informed him upon his arrival. "I'll see if she is available."

In short order, a well-groomed matronly woman with coiffed charcoal-colored hair and wearing an ankle-length burgundy dress joined him in the lounge area.

"I understand you're here regarding Vickie Murin," she said, slipping into the upholstered chair across from him.

"Yes, if I may, I would like to review the events immediately prior to her fatal accident. I'm particularly interested in talking to someone who last saw her the night of the incident."

"I was the last to see her," the stage manager said directly. "As I informed the accident investigators, it was following our

23

post-production party of The King and I. They are simple get-togethers, a way for the cast to unwind and share sentiments."

"Food and drink, I presume?" Adam asked.

"Yes---a buffet, along with some wine. If it's the alcohol you are concerned with, I can tell you Vickie had her usual single glass of wine."

"You sound definite in that regard."

"She never drank more in all the times I've seen her. In fact, I was told by the investigators her blood alcohol level did not exceed the legal limit. Is that not correct?"

"Correct," Adam said, glancing at the notepad he carried in hand. "You said you were the last to see her. How can you be sure of that?"

"Because I walked to her car with her following the party. I saw her get in and I saw her drive away."

"Was she wearing her seatbelt?"

"The stage manager furrowed her brow, "You know, I don't recall if she was. She could have attached it after I left her."

"But you did see her drive away?"

"Yes, from a distance."

"So everything was normal as far as you could tell?"

"Yes, except normally her husband would come and pick her up. She did not like to drive after dark. He was on duty, however, and unavailable."

"What frame of mind would you say Vickie was in?"

"Her usual...engaging and even tempered, though I doubt she would complain if something was bothering her. It's another example of her wanting to be nice by not pestering other people with her troubles. As with most of our actors, she viewed the stage as a way to come out of her shell...an opportunity to adopt a persona she might not otherwise put on display."

"A nice person," Adam proffered.

"Oh, I know nice when I see it, Mr. Fraley. Vickie cared for people. If I didn't have to get back to work, I could sit here for an hour and recite to you a litany of niceties associated with her," she said. "I work in a profession where I see plenty of the other. Believe me, Vickie was nice in every regard."

"Did she have a best friend?"

Garland struck a thoughtful pose. "You know, I'm not aware of a best friend she might have had. At least she never mentioned one to me. She worked part-time at a coffee shop. Between here and there, I'm sure she had plenty of acquaintances."

"She worked mornings at the coffee shop, I was told."

"Right...mornings at the coffee shop and evenings here when she was appearing in a show."

"And you never saw her recently upset for any reason?"

"As I mentioned, she was not the sort to burden others with her problems. She had her share, I'm sure, but it wasn't like she was suicidal or anything." The stage manager paused, as if debating whether to go on. "Having said this, there was one occasion a short while back when she expressed personal frustration which was quite unusual for her."

"Care to share it?" he asked.

"It doesn't have anything to do with the accident," she said.

"Investigators always like to have the total picture," he said. "They don't want to leave loose ends, no matter how irrelevant they may appear at the moment."

"Well, now that she's left us, I don't see any harm in it," she said before continuing. "As you may know, her husband was originally from Russia. For his last birthday, she bought a surprise gift for him...a puppy dog...a husky. It was as much for her as it was for him. His reaction, however, was not what she expected. 'This is no place to be raising a husky,' he apparently told her, and made her take it back. As you can imagine, she was upset. You know how it is when someone, especially a family member, outright rejects a gift of yours."

Adam nodded in agreement. "And to repeat...she left alone?" he asked.

"Yes. I held the car door open for her, since she had her hands full."

25

"Hands full of what?"

"Purse and pie."

"Pie?"

"Yes, one of Irma's pies...ever heard of them?"

"No."

"Irma's Pies is a boutique pie place over in Brandon. Her specialty is pumpkin-cheesecake pie with a bit of bourbon blended in. Vickie's husband loves pumpkin-cheesecake pie, so I bought her one to take to him. They come in an ornamental glass pie pan with the script IP logo etched into the bottom of the container. If you return the glass pan, you receive a discount on your next pie." She shook her head. "Lord knows where the pie ended up."

Adam checked his notes a second time.

"Mr. Fraley, may I ask you a completely unrelated question?" she asked, running her eyes over him.

"Sure."

The stage manager leaned forward in her chair as if to keep secret what she was about to say. "We find ourselves in a pickle here at the theater. We have a play opening up next week and one of our bit actors all of a sudden pulled out of his role due to a family emergency. He was slated to play a bartender as part of a background scene. He had no lines. His role called for him to make like he was serving drinks to a trio of young women hanging out at the bar. We're scrambling to find a replacement for him...."

Adam did not like where this was headed.

"...You have that engaging, Midwest manner about you..."

"Midwest Florida," Adam interjected. "I'm from the town of Strawberry Hills, a short distance northeast of here."

"Okay, Midwest Florida it is," she said. "You know we could exchange those denims of yours for a white shirt, black tie, black vest, black pants, and black shoes and you'd be stage ready. It might add some excitement to your life...not that you don't have enough already. It could also add a few extra dollars to your wallet."

Adam slowly looked up from his notes, unsure if she was joshing him or not.

"All the world may be a stage, Ms. Garland, but with apologies to the bard and you, I limit myself to the stage of everyday life. It holds enough excitement for me as is."

She leaned back and let out a sigh. "Well, it was worth a try."

"One last question," he said. "Did you mention the pie matter to the accident investigators?"

"No. It didn't cross my mind. What difference does it make? It's not like she feasted on a few pieces on the way home and zonked out on bourbon."

Adam smiled. "No, not likely."

•••

From the dinner theater Adam headed over to the accident scene to view it firsthand. Along the way, he reviewed in his mind the investigative report and the listing of items found in the vehicle. It was thorough all right, covering the contents of everything from the purse, to the glove compartment, to the trunk. Nothing in it, however, mentioning a pie and glass pan.

Following the same rural route Vickie Murin traveled, Adam slowed his pickup when nearing the accident scene. It was midday, yet the volume of traffic was exceptionally light, an indication of how thin it must have been the night of the accident.

He spotted the bridge in the distance and looked for skid marks till he was no more than twenty-five yards from the span. Eyeing none, he eased the pickup off the shoulder of the road, before pulling to a stop on a matted grass clearing. Hopping from his truck, he walked slowly toward the canal bank. He continued to look for skid marks, though aware any dirt tracks by now likely would have faded. Reaching the embankment he peered down the steep incline to the water's edge.

What to make of it? He turned and gazed up the road from whence he came. All signs seemed to support the investigators' conclusion. Vickie Murin, following a tiring evening, fell asleep at the wheel. She was not wearing a seatbelt. Was that not out of character for someone understandably concerned with road safety, Adam mused. Still, there was nothing to doubt regarding the official findings, except for the one thing they apparently didn't find…Irma's pie.

He trudged back to his truck and lifted a foot to climb aboard when he noticed a dark clayish substance on his shoe. He reached down and took a swipe at the stuff, running it under his nose. Wiping his fingers against his jeans, he decided one additional stop in his search was in order.

Adam drove his pickup nearly fifteen miles further north where the road merged with the interstate. Five more miles and he pulled into a truck stop, steering his vehicle alongside a dump truck driver snacking on a jumbo sandwich in his cab.

"Say there… mind if I ask you a question?" Adam called out to the burly man through his opened window.

"Go ahead," the driver mumbled through a mouthful of sandwich.

"Is there a mining company located in these parts?"

The driver nodded while gulping down his food. "There's a large one a bit north of here---MTS---Mine to Shore. They're a phosphate company. Why? You looking for a job?"

"Nah, I'm looking into an accident that happened a while back on a rural road south of here. I can't even tell you the road's name. I was just told how to get to it."

"Does it merge with the interstate?" the trucker asked.

"Yes."

"Around here it's called the Miner's Road," he quickly said. "I've traveled it a number of times when I was hauling phosphate years ago. Stuff is big business in this part of the state. The road's a favorite for truckers hauling to the port of Tampa…not much traffic and you avoid all the congestion on the interstate."

"You say this MTS outfit is a little north of here?"

28

"Yep. Take the next exit up and head inland for ten miles or so. You'll see it…big sign out front."

Adam bid his thanks and shortly was standing in the MTS front office facing a portly desk clerk wearing a visor and flashing a ready smile.

"I'd like to speak to the fleet manager," Adam politely requested.

"May I tell him what it is about?"

"Road accident," Adam replied with seriousness.

A few minutes later the clerk returned with the fleet manager in tow, a lanky fellow bearing a look of concern.

"Yes?" he said, placing his hands on the service counter.

"Sorry to bother you," Adam said, "but I'm investigating a fatal accident that happened back on the night of November 9th, on Miner's Road, I believe it is called.

"An accident involving us?" the fleet manager asked anxiously.

"No, not involving you. However, I understand your truckers travel the route frequently. I am curious if any of them might have seen something out of the ordinary the night of the incident."

Visibly relieved it was not one of his people involved in the accident, the manager adopted a more accommodating tone. "Hold on a minute," he said and disappeared into a side door.

Moments later he reappeared with what looked to be a large logbook. "What day did you say the accident was?"

November 9th---around midnight."

He flipped through the pages, running his finger down the list of entries, hesitating at two or three.

"Let's see…that was a Thursday night. There was one run that left at 8:10 p.m.," he said, glancing up at Adam.

"Too early," he replied.

The fleet manager resumed his scanning, stopping a half page further down. "Here's one with a 12:30 a.m. return time," he said. "The next departures and arrivals are not till 6:00 a.m."

"The 12:30 guy…any chance of talking to him?"

"Mort Sturgeon was the driver. Let me check on his whereabouts," he said, disappearing again.

"Well, it looks like you might be in luck," the manager said on his return. "He's scheduled to report in a half hour, if you care to wait."

"I'll wait," Adam said, and headed for a seat in the reception room.

He had picked through and browsed a variety of trucker magazines strewn across a coffee table when a husky voice commanded his attention. "You the fellow looking for me?" Adam looked up to see a man with the build to match the voice.

"If you're Mort Sturgeon, I am," Adam responded, rising to meet him. "Maybe your boss told you...I'm looking for information regarding a traffic accident down on Miner's Road back on the night of November 9th. I understand you were traveling the area at the time. Do you recall it?"

Sturgeon scratched at his chin stubble. "What night of the week was it?"

"Thursday night."

Sturgeon did some more scratching. "I do recall the run, but off hand I don't remember an accident. Whereabouts on the road was it?"

"Near a bridge fifteen miles south of the interstate. A car left the road and ended up in the river a block or so from the bridge, killing a young woman."

"Sorry, maybe I was early or late to it, but I recall no accident."

"Nothing out of the ordinary?"

Sturgeon shrugged. "Well...wait, I don't know whether you would call it out of the ordinary, but I do recall seeing an unmarked patrol car parked alongside the road not too far from the bridge."

"You sure it was an unmarked patrol car?"

"Son, any trucker who has traveled the number of miles I have would know what an unmarked patrol car looks like---

30

dark blue---antenna sticking out of the trunk---emergency lights on the side view mirror. Come to think of it, maybe he was there for an accident, though nothing else seemed to be going on except him parked there."

"Could be the investigation was over," Adam volunteered. "Did you get a look at him?"

"A glance. He appeared to be taking a break, munching away on something, probably a donut."

Or a piece of Irma's pumpkin-cheesecake pie, Adam thought.

Back at his office, Adam checked his contacts list. Under the entry for the sheriff's department there was a single listing dating back to the tenure of his old boss. The contact's name was Sydney Foster, a former sheriff's deputy who gave up his position to pursue a private sector career with Tampa-based Marlow International, a security firm specializing in the hush-hush world of corporate espionage. Adam recalled the day Foster dropped by the office for a social visit with his old boss. The three of them ended up going out to lunch together, at which time the ex-deputy instructed them on the fundamentals of private enterprise spying, from the pilfering of trade secrets to the prevention of eavesdropping. Upon hearing from Adam, Foster suggested an informal meeting prior to work. The next morning Adam walked the five blocks from his office to the Baylor Building, a mid-sized office tower housing the Marlow operation. A ground floor coffee shop checkered with chestnut brown tables squeezed within maroon walls served as the meeting locale. Amid the chatter of early morning patrons, Adam worked his way through the maze of people and furnishings to a corner table where Foster was already seated. A gangly fellow with closely cropped, rust-colored hair, he wore a corduroy jacket, blue shirt, and tan slacks. He stood to offer Adam a friendly greeting.

"So, how's Pete enjoying his retirement?" Foster asked, as a waitress poured them coffee. "He's enjoying it fine," Adam said, taking a seat at the table.

31

"Pete did me many a favor," Foster said. "He was one of my best contacts. I'm glad to hear I'm still on the list. I'll substitute your name for his, if you have no objection."

"It's a deal," Adam replied.

Foster took a sip of his coffee. "So, what can I do for you?"

"What can you tell me about a guy named Alex Murin? Are you acquainted with him from your days with the sheriff's department?"

"Yes, I am. He was, and I believe still is, a detective on the force. I had the occasion to work with him on a few cases, though generally our responsibilities took us in different directions. As a patrol deputy I generally traveled a separate path. However, there is overlap in the investigation process, so I came to know him, mainly on a professional level." Foster paused and leaned his arms on the table. "By the way, Adam, any information I give you is off the record. That's the understanding Pete and I had in sharing information. We also agreed not to discuss confidential matters. With that in mind, fire away. I'll let you know if it's something I am unable to discuss."

"Fair enough," Adam said. "On a professional level then, can you give me your opinion of him?"

Foster crossed his arms over his chest. "Well, I found Murin to be capable, competent, confident, and calculating. Lots of C's there but they best describe him. Also, he was more of an intellectual type than you normally find on the force. His record, at least while I was on board, earned him respect. The department is results oriented and he achieved results. By the time I left, he was considered one of the top detectives on the staff, if not the top one."

"A good cop." Adam said.

"Yes. A good cop."

"And on the personal side. A good guy?"

"A good cop...yes, but a good guy? I'm not sure I would attach that label to him."

"How about nice guy?" Adam asked.

32

"Nice is not the first word to come to mind, if I had to describe him. That's not to say he is a bad guy or a mean guy. I just don't know. Most of my interactions with him were on a professional level, though I was present at a few departmental social functions he also attended. He did strike me as a very motivated guy in whatever assignment he undertook." Foster paused to take another sip of coffee. "My father would always say much of life is learning to live with differences, especially among people. Because someone is different does not automatically mean they are inferior or better…just different. If you go through life thinking everyone should think and act the way you do, you are headed for heaps of frustration. I sensed this attitude in Murin. If you differed in ideas from him, you were inferior not only in your thoughts but as a person."

"Did not 'suffer fools gladly,'" Adam suggested.

"Exactly."

"Any other weaknesses worth noting?"

Foster thought a moment. "I don't know if you would describe it as a weakness, but he did give me the impression of a guy trying too hard to fit into the culture. As you probably know, he is originally from Russia. You can imagine how it is attempting to build up a support system from scratch. I had the feeling he was much more comfortable in his professional life than his personal one."

"He was married at the time?" Adam asked, knowing the answer.

"Yes, he was married. However, his wife was killed in an auto accident a while back. He took it hard from what I hear."

"Did you know her?"

"Met her at a few of the social functions. She was fairly attractive but seemed much more the introvert than he. I should add that Alex was a man who enjoyed the company of women. Not too surprising, considering he had star power and could get away with a little flirting here and there. From what I understand, he received as much as he gave. Nothing over the top, however, since the department frowned on it. Which

33

brings up another observation. Alex appeared to see life as a series of challenges and conquests whether professional or personal. If he walked into a bar, he was going to pick out the prettiest woman and have a go at her, the same as he would pick out the most challenging criminal case and have a crack at it. He was not going to settle for second best."

"An indication of his confidence level," Adam suggested.

"Definitely. Yet, he knew how to toe the line between confidence and blatant cockiness. The latter he held in check."

"How did he handle rejection?" Adam asked.

"Good question, to which I have no answer. The fact is I never saw Alex rejected in any professional capacity."

Foster checked his watch. "I'd better be getting to work. I hope this helps."

"I appreciate the input, Sydney," Adam said.

Foster dropped a couple of bills on the table to cover the tab. "One other thing. I don't know what this is all about nor do I necessarily care. All I'll say, if it was yours truly involved in some kind of law enforcement issue or conflict, I would not want Alex Murin on the opposing side. Take it for what it's worth."

"Understood," Adam said, bidding his contact a good day.

CHAPTER FOUR

Following a couple of weeks' worth of office orientation and training, Adam decided to ease his new employee into the fieldwork end of the business, starting with the Murin case.

"Why this case and what is it I'm to do?" Tamra asked in anticipation from across his desk.

"This morning I was bouncing around an idea regarding the case. We're at a crossroads stage where a decision needs to be made to press on with it or not. I'm not one to go past the point of diminishing returns in an investigation," he said, as though it was stated policy. "So far, all we have is a client who is suspicious of the way Vickie Murin died, a missing pumpkin-cheesecake pie, and an unmarked patrol car seen in the vicinity of the accident. As my former boss would say when faced with such evidence…all this does is raise the case to the level of a curiosity."

Adam looked to his office manager for a reaction but found none.

"What we are missing," he continued, "is a motive---a motive for murder."

"Perhaps he wanted the pie all to himself," she quipped.

Adam folded his arms and gazed past her in thought.

"Seriously, why not divorce her," she mused, "unless it was for insurance purposes."

"There was no insurance payout," he said, and left it at that, unwilling to divulge insider connections at this stage to the new hire whose loyalty had yet to be established.

"Another woman? Another man?" Tamra suggested with a shrug. "But then we're back to the divorce option," she added.

Adam unfolded his arms and set straight up in his chair. "The way Mr. Quigley describes her, she was not the type to be stepping out on him," he said, dismissing the notion. "Whether he was doing the stepping out is another matter. At this stage, there's no telling, which is why I've come up with an idea involving the combat duty I brought to your attention in the job interview."

Tamra shifted in her chair. If he did not have her full attention before, he had it now.

"There's a place not far from here called Orologio's. It's a combination bar and restaurant, one of those establishments where everything is fresh-faced, including the fixtures, the food, and the help. Heard of it?"

"Heard of it…never been there."

"It's also a favorite happy hour hangout for law enforcement types, including Alex Murin."

"How do you know?"

"By way of a tip from a fellow private eye. Last Friday evening I stopped in there for an early bird dinner. From my table I had a clear view of the bar area. Murin was among a handful of guys making merry for nearly an hour."

Adam reached for a folder on his desk and removed a photo of Murin. "Here is a stock photo of him taken from public records," he said, slipping it across the desk to her.

Tamra studied it for a moment before sliding it back. "Is this where I come in?" she asked.

"Yes. We need to engage him in conversation in an atmosphere where he may have his guard down."

"We?"

"You, to be precise, and, yes, for sexist reasons. Women are less likely to raise suspicions, even with Murin. He's not going to open up with a guy outside his circle. With you he would."

"Does he know you?" she asked.

"Unlikely. Even if he or one of his buddies did, they wouldn't associate you with me. Private investigators and cops normally don't pal around with each other. There are exceptions, but when it comes to business matters, we are often operating at cross-purposes."

"So, I'm to be the bait..."

"I prefer the word decoy," Adam interjected.

"Whichever," she said, brushing the distinction aside. "How do I engage him in conversation?"

"I'll leave that to your discretion, except to remind you we are after a motive."

"I go it alone?"

"Yes, though I will be there. Pick a bar stool and make like you are alone. If and when available, I will grab one next to you. However, I will keep my eyes glued to the TV mounted above the bar. We obviously will have no interest in each other."

"Obviously," she said. "The combat pay includes the drinks?"

"Full reimbursement, but not for any a guy may buy you."

"The one thing I will not do is wear any device---listening or camera," she said "I have issues with them."

Adam tumbled the response around his mind, debating whether to remind her this was a private investigation business. "Fair enough," he said, willing to let it pass. Nonetheless, he stood and swung open a vertical cabinet behind his desk. "You mean devices like these," he said and launched into a show and tell, picking out items one by one---miniature camera---listening device---and so on. "These are all samples collected by my former boss who never got around to using them."

"What's in the large bag?" she asked, nodding to an item shoved to the side.

Adam grabbed the container and placed it on the desk. "Believe it or not, this is a mobile phone with battery," he said, lifting the unit from the bag. "They are starting to make their way into the general population."

"People are going to lug that around?"

"Yeah, the size is the problem. Some outfit is coming out with a new model this year which folds into itself, so you can stick it into your pocket or purse. It will make this little dinosaur obsolete."

"I like the bag," Tamra said. "It's large enough to do something with."

"Want it?" he asked.

"Why not," she responded. "I can convert it into a woman's handbag and give the phone to my nephew to tinker with. He has a birthday coming up next month."

"All yours," Adam said, placing the phone back in the bag and closing the cabinet. "And you're right about the privacy issues. It's why the profession is also reluctant to utilize gadgetry, but for less noble reasons. They fear the civil laws far more than the moral ones. As for Orologio's, we will rely on your wiles."

"Today's Friday," she said expectantly.

"Sure is," he replied. "Take a couple of hours off early. I'll see you there at five."

She returned to her desk, cleaned it of loose paperwork, retrieved her purse from a drawer and left, flashing him a weak smile on her way out the door.

Adam's vision drifted to the photo of Murin. A handsome fellow, wise to the world no doubt, given his experience, which begged the question---where was the wisdom in matching his new hire up against him? By bringing in Tamra, he was upping the risk but the potential reward far exceeded any inherent risk, he believed. Furthermore, he had confidence in her, if for no other reason than the confidence she clearly exuded in herself.

He spent the remainder of the afternoon checking public records without adding much to what he already had compiled. Murin came to the States six years ago in 1983 and married one year later. Another year following his marriage, he landed a job as a detective with the sheriff's department. Shortly thereafter, he and his wife purchased a villa in Tampa's midtown section. Nowhere in the records was there mention of Murin receiving a reprimand of any sort. It all made the guy's life seem simple, at least the post-immigration phase. But we all know life is never simple, Adam reminded himself, when you start filling in the details, a few of which he was betting would surface before the night was out.

•••

Orologio's raised rectangular bar appeared like a well-lit stage centered above the surrounding dining area.

Adam arrived at five fifteen and entered, having spotted Tamra's silver Taurus sedan in the parking lot. Amid the chatter of patrons and clinking of glasses, he elbowed his way to the bar to find both of the key players in place. Tamra sat sidesaddle on a stool four down from where he stood. She had let her hair down, removed her glasses, and changed into a wine-colored dress matching the red wine she cradled in her hands. Meanwhile, Murin was bantering with his buddies across the way while occasionally surveying the bar. There was little doubt Murin was the Alpha male of the group, as the Betas jockeyed for position to pay heed to the detective who in his role as top dog projected the confident demeanor Sydney Foster spoke of.

A couple sitting next to Tamra rose to leave, allowing Adam to sidle onto a stool, his side to her back. He ordered a beer, keeping his eyes glued to the television monitor, as if the soccer match in progress halfway around the world was of greater interest to him than the proper yet alluring figure flying solo by his side.

"So, you look like you could use some company," came a hit from a would-be suitor approaching from the rear.

"Sorry, but its other company I'm expecting at any moment," came Tamra's frosty reply, slamming the door shut on the fellow before he had a chance to enter.

In short time, the pathways between the four-sided bar and brass railings ringing it were packed with a sizable contingent of the city's upwardly mobile seeking to make an impression on someone, preferably of the opposite sex.

The happy hour competition was in full swing, but just when the opportunity for a chance meeting between the leading

39

players in Adam's drama was close to being choked off by the gathering swarm, enchantment struck across the crowded room.

Adam caught Murin flashing a smile his way---Tamra's way to be precise. Eye contact had been made.

Murin disappeared into the crowd and reappeared a minute later at his office manager's side.

He extended his hand. "Hello, my name is Alex."

"Tamra," she said, accepting it.

"Tamra...short for Tamara...right?'

"Right."

"A good Russian name," he added.

His new hire wasted no time in grabbing hold of the opening.

"Is that a Russian accent I detect?" she asked in her velvety tone.

"Yes. I am originally from Irkutsk," he answered, as though she would know where the hell Irkutsk was.

"In southern Siberia---right?"

"Right you are," Murin replied.

"Near Lake Baikel."

"Right again," he said.

Adam was beginning to think his office manager had taken a crash course in Russian geography before she arrived. From the corner of his eye, he caught her brushing aside an unruly lock of hair from her face. "What brought you to the States?" she asked.

"What brings everyone here---opportunity."

"What do you do for a living?" she asked.

"Detective for the sheriff's department...and you?"

"I'm an office manager in a two-person office," she said matter-of-factly.

Adam braced himself for the follow-up question.

"You enjoy your work?" Murin asked, easing Adam's concern.

"You like it, if you like your boss."

"Makes sense. Two-person operation would put a premium on liking your boss. Do you?"

"He's tolerable."

"Meaning he's intolerable in some ways," Murin said, pursuing the point, much to Adam's dismay. "What are the intolerables?"

Tamra retrieved her wine glass from the bar to take a sip. "You might call him an office litterbug. He leaves water bottles---cups---papers scattered about."

"What else?" Murin asked, further irritating Adam.

"I've only been on the job a week but he frequently glances at me from across the room, as though I don't know what I'm doing."

"Maybe he's....

Tamra reached out to touch Murin's arm. "Oh, before you go on, there's one other intolerable I forgot to mention," she said, interrupting his thought. "The first thing every day he lifts my copy of the morning paper from my desk before I've had a chance to read it and takes it to his so he can check the sports scores. Sorry, what were you about to say about his checking on me from across the room?"

Murin smiled coyly. "I was going to suggest that maybe he's not checking on your work. Maybe he's checking out those legs of yours."

Wrong turn, Murin, Adam reckoned.

She let the remark pass.

"Sorry," Murin said, in reaction to her non-reaction. "I'm known to say what other men are thinking. The truth is I have much to learn about American women."

"And what have you learned so far?"

"No offense, but my former countrymen had a saying about American women...easy to bed, easier to wed"

And better dead, Adam said silently.

"You make it sound as simple as a nursery rhyme," Tamra said.

41

"Oh, I'll admit, they take some adjusting to," Murin continued.

"In what way?" she asked

"They are more finicky than Russian women...friendly but finicky."

Tamra turned to set her wine glass back on the bar. "Women who are finicky are not easy," she said, returning her attention to him.

"That smile you sent me across the way, it was intended to reel me in...for what?" he asked.

"Suppose I reel back the smile. You seem to have a bias against American women."

"Not when they're sexy smart," he said.

"When do we get to the smart part?" she asked

"Okay, on to the smart part. What was the last book you read?"

"Is this a test or an insult?"

"Neither. I'm trying to raise the level of discussion at your suggestion."

"Something tells me you did not fight your way through all this bar traffic to find out what the last book was I read," she said, motioning to the pressing multitude.

A champagne cork popped, igniting a roar from a group of revelers and a pause to the conversation. For a fleeting moment, Adam felt the kernel of a chemistry developing between the two---bad chemistry for sure, but for many women bad chemistry was better than no chemistry.

"So, how do you plan on finding a Russian woman in this country?" Tamra asked, as the din subsided.

"There's no need to," Murin said. "I've already made plans to bring one over from the mother country...my childhood sweetheart. She has grown into a very fine woman."

"You're planning to marry her?"

"Yes...I'll show you a photo of her."

Adam pictured Murin digging for his wallet and showing the photo to Tamra.

"Attractive," she said in a perfunctory manner. "Why did you wait this long to reconnect?"

"Complications," he said. "I---

Murin cut off the conversation, stepping back to make room for a group of his buddies who decided to join them.

"Say, Alex, aren't you going to introduce us," one of them crowed.

Adam rose to leave, a signal to Tamra their mission was over. With the two principals no longer alone, there was no sense in engaging in or listening to idle chitchat.

Back at the office awaiting her arrival, Adam contemplated bolder options to confirm his suspicions of Murin's guilt, ones involving risks possibly beyond the pale. None, however, satisfied him.

An hour passed before Tamra showed up at the office. Adam speculated on her having been engulfed in the scene, absorbed by the attention she was receiving.

"You did well," he said on her return, shelving his concern over the delay.

"I intended to get to his marriage," she said, "but the gang's arrival squelched the opportunity."

"We have it on record he was married," Adam said.

"Yes, but he may have let it slip what kind of marriage it was...solid or shaky."

"What was your overall impression of him?" Adam asked.

"He has a presence about him," she replied.

"Care to elaborate?"

"A disturbing presence," she responded.

"In what way," Adam asked, becoming a bit disturbed himself. "By disturbing, do you mean a good or bad presence?"

"Can't it be both?" she asked.

"How about you? What was your impression?"

"I think he's full of himself," he said, still pondering her good and bad presence observation.

"Meaning he's a murderer?" she asked.

"A conclusion we've yet to determine," he said. "But you did unearth a potential motive tonight."

"The other woman?"

"Yes. The photo he flashed you…how does she rate?"

"I suppose most men would consider her a knockout."

"Someone to kill for?"

"Yet to be determined, isn't it?"

Adam clasped his hands behind his neck and leaned back in his chair. "Let me throw this at you. Murin comes to the States on a green card. Decides he wants to become a citizen and to speed the process along, he charms an American woman into marrying him. He subsequently earns his citizenship and lands a job with the sheriff's department. His convenient marriage starts to sour and in the interim he somehow---somewhere--- reconnects with his childhood sweetheart, the love of his life. The rest is history."

"Again, why not a divorce?" Tamra asked.

"For a confident and calculating killer, a killing is cleaner and quicker. Murin had several factors operating in his favor. For one thing, as a member in good standing of a closed culture, he was above suspicion. Yes, he was the husband but there was no reason to believe the incident was anything other than an accident."

"Something to elicit an outpouring of support for him," Tamra interjected.

"Exactly, since there were no rumors of a troubled marriage for authorities to hang their hat on from what we know. And who knew what was going on behind the scenes in Russia? I'm sure he didn't spring the news of his old-new flame with colleagues until an appropriate grieving period had passed. Also, from what Quigley tells me, Vickie Murin was not the type to broadcast marital problems to others."

Tamra removed her glasses and set them aside. "So, what you're saying is we now have a potential motive but need the hard evidence to prove the accident was no accident."

"Yes, and tomorrow morning I plan on doing more digging," he said. "Set aside some time in the afternoon and we'll sit down and decide whether it is reasonable to proceed with this case."

•••

In the morning Adam drove to Irma's Pies, located within walking distance of the Starlight Theater. A quaint shop, it featured a large pumpkin-colored awning attached to a maize façade.

In response to Adam's query concerning the pie purchase, Irma assured him the man in the photo he was holding up to her had not returned a glass pie pan since the date of the accident. In fact, every pie container returned to her since the incident, was returned by regular patrons, each of whom she personally served. Upon his leaving, Irma also assured Adam she would notify him should the man in the photo show up with a returnable pan.

From Irma's, Adam headed to midtown Tampa, pulling his pickup to a stop in a quiet residential neighborhood lined with villa and condo complexes. Alex Murin's home stood a short distance from where he was parked, an attractive villa sporting a terracotta-tiled roof, a cognac-colored stone veneer exterior, and white stone walkway leading to a screened entry. Looming large on a well-manicured lawn was a date palm, freshly pruned and trimmed, its massive pineapple-shaped trunk capped by a crown of leaves.

Compared to Adam's spare lair in the in the lower middle class university section of town, it was clearly a step up in class. Perhaps someday he also might climb the economic ladder. In the meantime, he had another matter to tend to.

As he surveyed the surroundings, noting the innocent face of the neighborhood, he mulled over whether this was a case to be made or a case to be dismissed. He had already turned down a couple of potentially lucrative, far less risky cases, to devote time to this one. Was this good business practice he was engaging in? His thoughts drifted back to his client Charlton

45

Quigley. His former boss had advised him early on that every case reaches this stage and the decision to proceed or switch off the search engine invariably boils down to whether you believe in your client or not.

Adam started his engine and at once shut it off when he noticed a light brown van pulling into Murin's driveway. Along its side appeared the name "Molly's Maids" in yellow block lettering. He watched the driver unload a small cart of cleaning materials and wheel it to the screened entry where she retrieved a key from her brown uniform pocket and entered.

Adam observed the scene for a brief spell before igniting the engine again. Taking one more passing look at the Murin abode, he headed back to the office with both Irma's Pies and Molly's Maids on his mind.

•••

"So there you have it...the case thus far," Adam said, tossing the ball into Tamra's court.

"It's a start," she said.

"It's a start?"

"What do you want me to say...it's a middle...it's an ending?"

"What's your opinion of Charlton Quigley?" he asked.

"Based on what you told me and the one time he called..."

"He called?"

"Yes, to check on the progress of the case."

"Must have been a short conversation coming from your end, considering there's not much progress to report."

She gave him a perturbed look. "Yes, but a long enough conversation to say he strikes me as an honorable man."

Adam nodded his agreement. "Nonetheless, I need to do a background check on him."

"Really?"

"Yes. You always want to make sure your client actually has the relationship he claims he has with a subject. Nothing can sink a case quicker than to discover your client has an ulterior motive in seeking out your services. There have been instances where stalkers have hired private investigators to track down targets of theirs with bad consequences. In one case a woman ended up getting murdered. You can imagine the vulnerable state the investigator was left in."

"But the target in this case is not a woman."

"No, but it's just good policy to touch all bases," Adam said.

"I still say he's an honorable man even without the benefit of a background check."

"In all probability you're right," he said. "Listen, I've been weighing our next step, one that could determine whether we continue or not, one that raises the risk factor."

"And the combat pay?"

Adam smiled. "You're getting ahead of me."

Tamra angled her head at him in anticipation. "But you're correct," Adam continued. "It calls for your skills. And before I launch into the details, I will remind you of your veto power."

"I don't need reminding. I keep the option at the ready since Orologio's."

Adam scooted his chair closer to the desk and looked Tamra straight in the eye. "Okay, here it is. We need one solid piece of evidence to convince us it's worthwhile to carry on with the case. This afternoon, on my way back from Irma's Pies, I stopped by Murin's home in the midtown district to check out his residence. As I was about to leave, a Molly's Maids van pulled into his drive." Adam detected in his office manager's eyes her growing realization as to where this was headed. "The arrival of the cleaning service gave me an idea on how we may gain access to the home."

"For what?" she immediately asked.

"The glass pie pan. If it's there, it is a direct piece of evidence Murin was present at his wife's death. Who else would have taken it from the scene?"

"What makes you think he still has it in his possession?"

"There's a reasonable chance he stored it away until he's ready to go in for a refill. Remember, as a detective he's aware of crime scene protocol and police follow-up. No doubt he has seen the accident report. There's no mention of the pie in it, so as far as he's concerned, the empty container is of no consequence."

"Why not wait until he goes in for the refill?"

"Several reasons. One, it would be better to find it in his residence. Two, there is the uncertainty he will return it. Three, I don't know if I can count on Irma as much as I can count on you."

"How do you propose to find out if it's there? Certainly, you are not considering a break-in?"

"Here's what I'm considering. Earlier I called Molly's Maids to find out if they have any openings for their cleaning crews. They do."

Adam sensed his office manager was now fully aware of what he was about to propose. "The cleaning crews are almost exclusively made up of female workers. I am positive of it. So what we need is a woman to immediately apply for a position."

Tamra took a slow, exaggerated glance over her shoulder, as if to see if another woman was in the room. "You said this move called for my skills. Did you mean cleaning skills and, if so, what makes you think I possess them?"

"I'm referring to your skills of observation," he replied.

Adam continued. "I don't expect this woman to take the long shot gamble of being assigned Murin's home. Nor do we want to wait around for the assignment to take place. It could take weeks...even months."

"Suppose she seeks the assignment?" Tamra asked.

"Could still take weeks or months. No, what I'm thinking is once she gets on board, she at once volunteers to trail a regular worker around on one of her assignments as a preliminary training exercise. And since the new hire lives close to the Murin home, it would be very convenient to have her introductory lesson there."

"And then what?" Tamra asked.

"She gains entry into the residence and in so doing launches into a search for the pie pan while ostensibly assisting the regular worker."

"And if by some miracle she spots the pie pan, she absconds with it?" Tamra asked. "Can illegally obtained evidence be entered into court?"

"Good question and it's why we have to murky up the legal waters a bit," he replied. "If she locates the pie pan, she stuffs it into a trash bag, one nearly full, which she will load into the trash cart. It so happens the regular cleaning lady performs her duty the day before trash pickup. Once the pan is in the bag and in the cart, our insider's work is completed. She goes back to the company to inform them she really isn't cut out for this kind of work and resigns before she even gets started."

"And the trash?"

"I'm betting Murin puts it out for pickup either the night before or early the next morning before he takes off for work."

"And you go trash hunting?"

"Correct. Once something is removed from a house as trash, it no longer is a case of theft. The item becomes public property. I admit there are some gray areas here but it does not easily fit the definition of burglary. The argument can be made it is not a forcible entry. It definitely would be difficult to prove it was. Besides, is Murin going to file a burglary report and turn the spotlight on the pie pan? I don't think so."

"More like a conspiracy to commit burglary," she pointed out.

"For a pie pan?" Adam said. "Petty theft at worst. Listen…"

"I'll do it," she said, cutting him off.

"You're sure?" he asked, surprised at the quick response.

"How can I pass up more combat pay?"

"That's your sole reason…more pay? Adam asked.

"I have my reasons. One…my boss is proposing it. Two…the extra pay. Three…to find out if the man is really a legitimate suspect."

Adam hesitated. "Okay, call Molly's Maids and let's get the ball rolling," he said, shoving his chair from the desk to signal the end of the discussion.

Later in the day he did some background checking on Charlton Quigley. As expected, he was found to have a clean record both as a civilian and military man. The marine stint included the awarding of a Bronze Star and Purple Heart. At the end of the day, Adam dropped by the coffee shop frequented by Quigley where an accommodating manager confirmed he was a regular and that Vickie Murin very much enjoyed his company while on break.

The following week Tamra was hired by Molly's Maids, the process expedited due to the firm's critical shortage of help. As soon as she signed on, she made a modest request to the manager. Prior to her first assignment, would it be possible to tag along with a colleague to get a feel for the job...on her own time of course. She already had asked a co-worker if she minded and was told by the regular she would be glad to have her follow along. Why not, the manager responded, reminding her it would be on her own time.

The speed with which the plan was proceeding allowed scant time for Adam to engage in his favorite pastime of second guessing himself. Nonetheless, one observation hung like a signpost in the back of his mind, shadowing his every thought. Was he taking advantage of the new hire? Exploiting her enthusiasm in an effort to make case? He remembered what his former boss advised on his way out the door to retirement, when you're allocating risk, the lion's share goes to you. Thus far it was more like the lamb's share. Still, what was he to do with the resources at hand? The job called for a woman and she fit the bill, he reasoned. When in doubt, go with your gut, another of his mentor's favorite maxims. However, the risk was escalating along with the doubt, and the two made for a very combustible combination.

CHAPTER FIVE

A mid-afternoon haze hung over the Midtown neighborhood sealing the stillness below. A half-block down from the Murin home, Adam sat slouched behind the wheel of a brown sedan rental car tucked between two other bland sedans.

Presently, the staccato burps of a trombone blew through the opened window of a nearby home, reverberating up and down the street, puncturing the peaceful atmosphere. It required a few minutes of stakeout time for Adam to identify the tune as Seventy-Six Trombones, the requisite number of the instruments it would take to drown out the discordant notes he was attempting to tune out without much success. That was until the Molly's Maids van showed itself on the scene, crawling up the far end of the street and turning into Murin's driveway.

A plump, flaxen-haired woman climbed from the van, followed by Tamra from the passenger side. Both wore bulky brown uniforms and hairnets. Tamra had shed her glasses, donned a tawny colored wig, and appeared a different woman from afar. She calmly trailed the driver to the entryway, waited for her to unlock the door and followed her inside.

Adam checked his watch. At 1:30 p.m., his office manager was behind enemy lines.

The burps from the trombone rejoined his consciousness like unwanted noise to a tinnitus sufferer. Nonetheless, it represented a return to normalcy, which is all he was asking for at the moment. Another hour and the caper would be completed, successfully or not.

Adam played the countdown game in hopes of hurrying the clock along before something unexpected happened. With each passing minute, however, his concern eased. The plane was on final approach, the train pulling into the station, the ship sailing into harbor. Shortly, it would be welcome back time.

At 2:20 p.m. the music ended, bringing a peace back to the neighborhood. The anxiety filling him waned, replaced by an anticipation of his employee's return, of evidence uncovered, of a case invigorated. What he didn't anticipate was the sheriff's vehicle cruising up the far end of the street and pulling curbside at the Murin household.

"Christ!" Adam snapped, striking the dashboard with his fist. A jumble of thoughts rushed through his mind as the trombone burps resumed. He asked himself, where in the jumble was the backup plan? He knew full well there was none.

•••

Tamra performed the puppy routine, following on the heels of her trainer Dolores, occasionally peeking in and out of drawers, cupboards, and closets when out of her sight, and with no luck. Admittedly, her attention was immediately stolen upon entering by the stark contrast of the villa's interior with its exterior. Off-white hues prevailed throughout the inside, serving as background for large, framed black-and-white photographs of snow-covered woodlands and stylish women, bundled up from head to foot, strolling brightly lit city streets. Among the photographs was the same one Murin had shown her in the bar, of the girlfriend posing under a streetlight, prominently displayed on the homeowner's bedroom wall.

The black and white scheme was broken by Murin's personal library to which an entire wall of the living room was devoted. Tamra took a dust rag to the dark wooden shelves, availing herself of the opportunity to browse the collection. Arranged by subject the volumes were almost exclusively works of Russian authors, Turgenev, Tolstoy, Pushkin, Chekov, Solzhenitsyn, Dostoevsky, Pasternak, along with works of less renowned authors. Plenty of tortured souls here, she mused. A sprinkling of trade publications on police procedures, crime scene techniques, and Florida statutes were included. Tamra believed the entire collection was a testimony to Murin's roots and contributed greatly to the villa's exterior-interior divide.

"That's about it," Dolores said to her in broken English, as the two sat in the living room on a charcoal leather couch going over the checklist following the cleaning.

"I'm going to take one more quick look at the kitchen," Tamra said, anxious at the thought of leaving empty-handed.

Dolores shrugged. "Sure."

Tamra started on the cupboards, opening and closing doors in rapid succession. All items were clean and in proper order. Not until she reached a bottom corner cabinet, crammed with miscellaneous utensils did her interest peak. Picking her way through graters, slicing boards, measuring cups, roasting pans, pasta strainers, and cake pans, she came upon the glass pie pan she at once recognized as the prize. Carefully sliding it out from under the pile, she stood and checked its bottom, noting the Irma's Pies logo. In the same moment she caught from the corner of her eye Dolores moving toward a front bay window. Through the opening Tamra spotted a sheriff's car parked at the curb.

"Mr. Murin's home early," Dolores said, moving away from the window.

Tamra snatched the pie pan and carefully placed it in a plastic trash bag along with the other trash. She next slipped the sanitary gloves she was wearing from her hands and deposited them in the container. She then grabbed a handful of paper towels from a roll mounted above the kitchen counter and stuffed them on top of the haul.

Murin strode through the front door and stood in the living room with hands on hips. "About finished?" he asked in a commanding tone.

"Yes, we are finished," Dolores replied in a compliant manner.

Tamra kept her back to the living room, taking her time in tying the knot on the trash bag.

"What are two of you doing here today?" Murin asked.

Tamra felt the weight of his eyes on her back.

"She's a trainee," Dolores replied. "She's learning the procedures."

Out of the corner of her eye, Tamra caught Murin taking a step toward the kitchen. She realized there was no way she would be able to avoid eye contact, an occurrence sure to fire an immediate recognition of her. What was the object at Orologio's had presently become the peril. She could feel his breath at her back when the ear-splitting sound of screeching automobile tires halted him in his tracks. Instantly, he did an about face and headed for the window to see what all the commotion was about.

From the kitchen Tamra momentarily had a clear view of the street. Some guy in a late model sedan was burning rubber up and down the road, executing donuts with the precision of a winning racecar driver.

"What the hell!" Murin exclaimed, darting from the window to the front door.

Tamra seized her opportunity, slipping out the door a moment after Murin. She stepped briskly to the side of the villa to the parked mobile storage bin, deposited the bag containing the pie pan, and returned to the van to await Dolores. Meanwhile, a strong scent of burned rubber lingered in the air, as the irate homeowner continued to glare up the street at the disappearing motorist. From the look on his face, Murin appeared to be debating whether to take out after the showboat. Instead, he turned back to the house, running into Dolores at the entranceway. For a minute the two spoke, each glancing several times at Tamra sitting demurely in the van. Surely he did not recognize her, she reassured herself. At last, Dolores broke away, joining her in the van for the ride back to the office.

"Was Mr. Murin upset about something?" Tamra asked innocently.

"No, he was asking me to alert him beforehand if anyone other than me would be working in the house."

The moment they were clear of the property, Tamra breathed a sigh of relief.

•••

"I'll repeat what I told you over the phone last night...good thing you did have a backup plan," Tamra said, teasing him with a smile from across the room.

Adam reached into the bottom drawer of his desk and pulled out the baggy containing the glass pie pan.

"Did you have any problem fishing it out?" she asked.

"None," he said, slipping it from the bag. "Murin wheeled the bin out for curbside pickup before he headed for work. It took about fifteen seconds for me to drive up and grab it. Good job, Tamra."

She nodded her appreciation.

"Did your co-worker have anything to add regarding Murin...or his former wife, or whatever?"

"She was tight-lipped the entire way, particularly after I told her on the ride back to the office I was submitting my resignation, since I wasn't sure from the start this was the sort of work I would enjoy. As if anyone would be overjoyed with it," she added.

"Anything inside the home catch your attention?"

"Plenty of stark black and white Russian landscape photos decking the walls and halls, along with a few city street scenes, plus a large photo of the girl he left behind. He also has a nice personal library, mostly Russian literature. Overall, I'd say it was a Spartan atmosphere---clean and orderly with a bold masculine flavor."

Adam held her eyes for a moment. The twinkle in them, spontaneous or not, did not escape him. "Thank you for the insight."

"Like I told you," she said. "He has a presence about him."

"Any mementoes of his former wife?"

"None I noticed."

Adam glanced down at the pie pan he had slipped from the bag.

"What next?" she asked.

"An appointment with the district attorney's office to give them what we got."

"Is it enough, though?" she asked.

"Enough to perk up their ears," he answered.

•••

Assistant District Attorney Rusty Daniels, a squat, freckle-faced redhead, dressed in a rumpled blue suit was assigned to hear Adam out. Daniels escorted him to a compact, windowless office cubicle, indicating to Adam the degree of importance the D. A. was bestowing on the meeting.

"What have you got?" Daniels asked right off.

Adam presented his case, from Mr. Quigley's suspicions, to the presence of the unmarked sheriff's car in the vicinity of the accident scene, to the missing pie pan, to the unfastened seatbelt, to the girlfriend waiting back in Russia.

For the most part Daniels appeared attentive, several times interlacing his stubby fingers beneath his chin and eyeing him directly, at other times nodding thoughtfully.

When Adam finished Daniels took a deep breath, clasped his hands on the desk, and again locked eyes with him. "Okay, here's what we got," he said. "One…an elderly gentleman suspicious of the wife's death, for no solid reason I might add. Two, a missing pie pan…"

"As I said, it is no longer missing," Adam interrupted. "It was in the Murin home. It is a direct link between him and the accident scene."

"Other than your word, what proof is there the pan came from his home?'

Adam handed over the bag containing the pan. "You might want to check it for fingerprints. I'm sure his are on file at the sheriff's department."

"May I ask---how did you come into possession of it?" Daniels asked.

"Through some trickery."

Daniels eyed him skeptically.

"Legal trickery," Adam added.

"And is there definitive proof it is the same pan supposedly in the car? Who's to say he didn't make a trip to Irma's Pies to purchase one on his own?"

"Irma says so," Adam pointedly replied.

"Or someone else purchased one for him at another time," Daniels suggested.

"Unlikely," Adam countered. "And what about the unfastened seatbelt...also suspicious, don't you agree, considering her concern with car safety?"

"It cuts both ways, Fraley. Don't you think a smart detective would know enough to fasten her seatbelt if he was concocting the scheme you suggest?"

"Not if he thought it would raise questions on how she suffered that hard of a blow to the head."

Daniels dismissed the point with the shake of his head. "Mr. Fraley, Vickie Murin's best friend was a young woman by the name of Betsy Reynolds. How do I know? I know it because I was assigned to the accident case. The department was considering the option of bringing up manslaughter charges against the drunk driver. During the course of the investigation, we learned the car the women were riding in caught fire immediately upon impact. Vickie was able to escape the vehicle. Betsy, the driver, was not so fortunate. The seatbelt she was wearing malfunctioned and she became trapped in the conflagration. She died on the scene." Daniels eyes sunk deep into Adam. "I'm all for buckling up," Mr. Fraley, "but does this give good reason why she may not have been wearing her seatbelt?"

"I'd still bet on it," Adam said, though he admitted to himself that the probability just lessened.

"As for the unmarked car," Daniels continued, "the sheriff's people have some latitude on their use. It could have been parked there for any number of reasons."

"Coincidental, are you saying?"

"I'm saying everything you have is coincidental." The Assistant District Attorney leaned forward. "This isn't the fun and games you seem to be playing here, Mr. Fraley. It's a sheriff's detective we're talking about for God's sake. And what is his motive? The fact an elderly man repeats to you a remark the wife made indicating some dissatisfaction with the marriage is hardly motivation for murder. If the marriage was on the rocks and he detested her, why not get a divorce?"

"With all due respect, Mr. Daniels, do you know how many spouse killers that could be asked of?" Adam countered.

Daniels nodded, granting the point, leading Adam to pounce on the motive angle. "He didn't want a messy divorce that would drag out over time. He wanted a quick, clean break to clear the path for his girlfriend to rejoin him in the States. I'm guessing he married his first wife to smooth his path to citizenship. Now he's cleared the path completely and in the process, generated a boatload of sympathy for his loss, I'm sure. The guy is brimming with confidence. He thinks he can get away with murder and thus far it looks as though he may have."

Daniels rose to his feet and put it to him squarely. "Sorry, Mr. Fraley," he said. "It requires much more solid evidence to bring a charge, a murder charge no less, against a sheriff's detective in good standing with the department, which counters the official accident report. What you have now adds up to no case."

•••

Adam cast a forlorn look across the desk at his office manager. "Can't say I disagree all that much with what he said."

"Did you raise any suspicions in him at all?" Tamra asked.

"Difficult to say. What I did do is bring it to his attention. He is now subject to being asked the question 'what do you know and when did you know it' should a murder case eventually come to light. It's part of his responsibility to make judgments that won't come back to haunt him and the D.A.'s office."

"Or to bring cases that would do the same," Tamra added.

Adam managed a fleeting smile. "Right."

"Shall we put it on hold, like we've done with our other cases while we've dealt with this?" she asked.

"You mean all those employee background checks, cheating spouse requests, kids doing drugs, and so on?" Adam asked derisively.

"Yes," she answered. "By the way, you have a special visitor coming in to see you in a few minutes."

"Oh yeah? Who might that be?"

"Your former boss."

"Really? What's he doing here?"

"He said he's passing through town and had a lengthy airport layover, so at the last minute he decided to book a rental car and make a quick visit."

"Where is he?"

"He ran down the street to say hello to his old barber. He should be back shortly. Meanwhile, I need to make a visit to the bank to make a deposit," she said, retrieving her purse from a drawer. "You two have fun with the good old days."

•••

"Before I give you my opinion on what sounds like the case of the missing pie, let me compliment you on your taste in office managers," Pete Peterson said. "It's far better than mine."

"Thanks, I think," Adam said.

Peterson was stretched out in a chair, his hands clasped across his spindly frame, legs crossed at the ankles. He wore an off-white shirt and matching slacks. A straw hat covered silken gray hair hanging to the base of his neck. Above all, Adam noticed the taut, leathered face sporting a deeper tan and cheeks more hollow than he could recall.

Appearing comfortable in his old surroundings, Peterson removed the hat and plopped it on Adam's desk. "I still think you should get a macaw for this place," he said, surveying the scene. "If nothing else, it would keep you from dozing off following those all-night stakeouts."

"I'll see if I can work it into the budget," Adam said. "How's Jill?"

"Doing fine. She's totally submerged in the business."

"How in the hell did you ever manage to rope her into marrying you? She must have been in big demand."

"Patience. I was like the item in the store a woman makes a mental note of when shopping with the idea of returning to it in case she doesn't find anything better. Needless to say, she returned."

"Is the scrimshaw trade holding up?"

"Holding up well, but ever since Mel Fisher raised the Spanish galleon Atocha from the dead, everyone's into treasure hunting. Now all sorts of strange items keep popping up, some of which we add to inventory, others...not. It's similar to this business. You have to separate the real from the fake. It's to the point where a certificate of authenticity is required for the certificate of authenticity."

"About the Murin case, Pete," Adam said, redirecting him to the original topic. "Like I said, it was no accident."

"You remind me of a loss prevention specialist I locked horns with on a case a longtime back," Peterson said. "He was continually trying to convince everyone, including me, how there was no such thing as an accident. Every crash or whatever could have been prevented, so why call it an accident, he would ask. 'So why was the word in the dictionary' I asked him in return every time he brought the issue up."

"This has more to do with intentions, Pete. You can't leave those out of the equation when it comes to accidents."

"Exactly what I pointed out to the loss prevention guy. 'Unintentional is also in the dictionary. Do you want to take that word out too?' I asked him. Which brings up the matter of unintended consequences." Peterson straightened in his chair. "You're not going to care for what I'm about to say, Adam. Put simply, you don't have a lot to hang your hat on, if you wore one. The Orologio's Restaurant gambit was an okay move, but the house caper was beyond foolish...more like farcical. The consequences could have been severe."

"It gained us evidence," Adam responded.

"Remember all those occasions when I'd continually stress the importance of weighing the risk against the reward? Well, was the potential evidence in this instance worth the risk? Not in my opinion and I've always considered myself a risk taker, as you well know. Private investigators walk around with one foot in legal land, the other toeing illegal terrain. It's like an endless game of hopscotch, where you attempt to keep your balance while picking up pieces of evidence."

"I considered dropping an anonymous tip to Internal Affairs," Adam said.

"With what you've got? All that'll get you is some blowback, which you'll probably be getting somewhere down the line anyway."

"What would you recommend as a next move?" Adam asked.

Peterson grimaced. "Sorry, my friend. You're now the boss and mastermind. You draw up the strategies and make the decisions."

"How about some direction then?"

"In all seriousness, if there's anything worse than a cop killer, it's a killer cop. For this one you go the extra mile...to the ends of the earth, if necessary. Just keep from falling off it," Peterson said. "Look, words are important to me as you've heard me say countless times. Long before you came on board with me, I had a case involving a city detective. His wife suspected him of cheating on her. They had two girls, nine and eleven. He was clever in his treachery but not so his paramour. She kept a journal detailing every tryst, including time and place. Somehow I became aware of it and later in possession of it..."

"Surely, not through poaching, Pete."

"Clandestine activity is how I would describe it. Anyway, the times and places matched up with his whereabouts."

"Did they split?"

"Yes. I was the one who confronted him with the evidence. He shrugged it off as though it was to be expected, like, you know, those things happen; they're personal matters. In my opinion, he was not only cheating on his wife but also on the girls..." Peterson paused. "On my nieces, to be specific," he said, pointing to his chest.

Adam flinched in surprise. "It's your sister Rachel you're talking about?"

"Yes, my sister Rachel. I understand there are levels of crime---gradations you might say---but the vow breakers are like the oath breakers. I never did buy into the 'words-will-never-hurt-me' line. Give me the broken bones. Thirty years later, what are you going to remember...the broken bones or the broken words?"

"No wonder you've got that go-get him look in your eye," Adam said.

Peterson again stretched out his frame. "Are you still living in that cubbyhole of an apartment?"

"Yeah, but I'm looking to move closer to the downtown area. I've been keeping my eye out for a loft."

"Why a loft?"

"The personal computer is making it easier to work from home and a loft gives you enough space for separate office and living quarters, as well as separate entrances and exits. Plus, I'd also be doing away with one of the rental checks I'm now writing."

"You want shady strangers coming into your home or knowing where you are living?"

"If I recall right, Pete, you conducted some of your business from home."

"You may also recall it was on a very selective basis and my official office was right here where we are sitting," Peterson replied. "Keep in mind, you may have to get a loft in a commercial zone if you're planning on running a business office out of it."

"Good point," Adam said.

"And how's that former instructor of yours doing, the one you were working with on the Sunshine Skyway Bridge case? You still carrying the torch for her?"

Adam managed a weak smile. "In plain speak, we are no longer an item. She presently is my academic advisor, though she also serves as my advisor in life."

Peterson grinned. "It comes as no surprise. She's a classy woman from what I recall and doubtlessly out of your league--- culturally speaking, of course. As much as you like to throw out a Shakespeare quote now and then, you're more a man of the people."

"So was he."

"You know what I'm getting at. You're not programmed to hang out in faculty lounges solving the world's problems. You're a son-of-the-soil guy from Strawberry Hills, Florida, who probably belongs back in his little hometown."

"Now you tell me. And what exactly would I be doing in Strawberry Hills?"

"I don't know…eating your mother's strawberry shortcake while watching the berries grow. How are your parents?"

"They're fine. Still enjoying each other's company."

"I've got one other question before I leave. Was it your guy Shakespeare who said something about all of us trailing clouds of glory when we enter the world? It's the one line I remember from my school days."

"I believe it comes from another William. William Wordsworth. If I'm not mistaken, the line is "trailing clouds of glory do we come.""

"So, it's another William. Even so, I still like it…the image of the trailing clouds, what it represents. Unfortunately, my trail of clouds is thinning out, except for the ones in my eyes."

Peterson grabbed his hat from Adam's desk. "Well, time for me to go before I start picking up the phone and dialing for leads."

"Miss you around here, Pete."

His old boss said nothing. He didn't need to. The winsome look said it all.

•••

"You're not sure of his guilt, are you?" Adam asked straight out.

"I have to be honest, Adam. I'm not sure at all," Tamra replied. "It appears to be a very shaky case. What did Mr. Peterson think? Did you ask him?"

"He agrees with you."

"The question is where we go from here, if anywhere?" she asked.

Adam was not about to let go. "To the ends of the earth," he said. "Where did Murin say he was from in Russia?"

"Irkutsk. It's in Southern Siberia."

Adam grabbed his water bottle from the desk and took a drink. "You know, years ago I watched a program on public television devoted entirely to the Trans-Siberian Railroad. They took viewers along the complete route from Moscow to Vladivastak. And not long after, I saw Doctor Zhivago and Julie Christie and said right then and there I'm going to take that trip someday." He paused to take another swig of water. "Do you know if Irkutsk is on the Trans-Siberian route?"

Tamra glanced up from a handful of mail she was sorting. "Yes, I believe so…this isn't headed where I think it's headed, is it?"

"Tell me, when did you become an authority on all things Russian?" he asked.

"I'm far from an authority. However, I have read on travel there. It also was once on my list of places to see."

"Well, I've come to the belief the truth lies somewhere back in Murin's old home town," he said.

"So, you're going to take a trip to Russia?" she asked in somewhat disbelief.

"A working vacation is how I see it."

"Adam, what convinces you he had a hand in his wife's death, to the point of making you travel halfway around the world to help prove it?"

"I have a nose for guilt. I can sniff it."

"Perhaps the sheriff's department might want you for their canine unit."

He let the comment pass. "Yeah, I can't help but believe the evidence we need is rooted back in Murin's old stomping grounds and the person who holds the key to it is his lady friend. No doubt there was correspondence between the two, but we're not going to gain access to it here without a court order."

"You're suggesting she's a co-conspirator?" Tamra asked. "In what way?"

"By pressuring him to make the break. There's even the chance she had prior knowledge of the fake accident plan," Adam said. "Book me on a flight to Moscow ASAP and get me a visa. I understand you can obtain one much faster if you go through Russian government channels."

"Adam, why not contact an overseas private investigator? Can't they do the checking for you?"

"Not with this case. I wouldn't trust them with a missing person case, much less a potential homicide."

"But this is a missing person case, isn't it? You're trying to find the girlfriend."

"Finding her is one thing. Analyzing her is another. There is no substitute for one-on-one contact in taking the measure of a person. I'm as interested in what's off the official record as in what's on it."

"Then I suggest you also get a guide. You are not going to get far on da and nyet.

"Do you have one to recommend?" he asked in half jest.

"No, but I can check to see if one's available."

"Before you do, let me touch base with my advisor at school. They have overseas connections and she might have a personal recommendation. As a matter of fact, hold off on the visa hunt till I speak with her. The school may be able to expedite matters."

"She's your travel advisor as well as your school advisor?"

"Also a crush of mine sometime back," he said, wishing he hadn't.

"What happened?" Tamra asked.

"I grew up."

"And she didn't?"

"She was already grown," Adam said.

"I don't understand," Tamra said, pushing it.

"I spent a four-year hitch in the military. Following my discharge I attended college on the G. I. Bill. Don't ask why but I majored in English Literature, not knowing what the hell I was going to do with the degree. I wasn't interested in teaching or writing and what else was I to do? I was one of the many students who could not settle on a career so I bounced back and forth between disciplines. It so happened I ended up working in your position for my former boss while attending school. He was on the lookout for someone with research skills and those I had. As I gathered experience I also gained interest in the field, so I decided to add a second degree in criminal justice."

"You need a degree to be a private investigator?" she asked.

"No, but it doesn't hurt to have one, especially when it comes to sorting out legal issues."

"And what role did your advisor play during all of this?" she asked.

"She played the adult, directing and re-directing my interests and abilities as best she could. She also helped me on a case Pete and I were working on."

"And therein was born your interest in her," Tamra said flat out.

"Through all my indecision and procrastination, we spent an inordinate amount of time together hashing things out. We also discovered in the process we had much in common. In the end, however, she convinced me I would not be the same man I was five years down the road. She was right. I'm not."

Adam snatched his desk calendar and examined it, ending the reminiscing. "Well, I've always claimed to be a spontaneous travel kind of guy, but this Russian journey may be stretching the definition."

"You think?" she said.

CHAPTER SIX

She wore a clinging, floral-patterned skirt of pastel shades with a slit that rose thigh-high on a crossed leg, exposing sinewy muscles down to the toes on which she balanced a flip-flop.

From across the room, Adam indulgently observed the manner in which she would alternately cross legs, uncross them, cover them, and with a sleight of hand uncover them in a ritual as precise as a hitter's before he stepped into the batter's box.

On one occasion she interrupted her routine, removing her glasses to glance across the room, catching Adam's eye, a hard expression forming on her face. Adam smiled, hardening it further.

He returned to minding his own business, gathering his test papers together after scanning them a final time. He carried the stack to the front of the classroom, depositing them on the instructor's desk. As he exited the room, he took a last sidelong glance at the leg crosser, drawing another glare from her.

Once outside he strode to the far end of the hallway to the office of his academic advisor, Nancy Egan, finding her at her desk. "Do you know a Julie Hamilton?" he asked, sliding into a chair.

"Yes, I am also her advisor," the mannered woman in the smart, tawny colored suit replied. "She happens to be the daughter of the vice-chancellor and the second leading scorer on our women's basketball team. They've advanced to the

Southeast Regional Tournament finals in case you didn't know. It's quite the story."

"Impressive," Adam said. "Did you also know she is a cheat?"

She tilted her head in surprise. "How so?"

"For the last hour I witnessed her in action. She utilizes those long legs of hers…thighs in particular…as a crib sheet, scribbling notes on them in invisible ink."

His advisor creased her brow. "Invisible?"

"Not invisible to her. She has a pair of specially made glasses to read the ink."

"Are you sure?"

"Ninety-five percent sure."

"Did you bring it to the attention of your instructor?"

"Mister mild and meek Horace Galenty? What's he going to do? Run over and grab her glasses, throw them on, and ask her to spread her legs so he can take a gander? You know what kind of hot water that would land him in. Nope, she will waltz on out taking the evidence with her."

She sighed her assent. "I'm afraid you're right. She easily could counter his charge with a claim of sexual harassment."

"A leg-leering professor," Adam suggested.

"Sadly, students are very aware of how much they can get away with when it comes to certain teachers. Has she developed a classroom rapport with Galenty, as I suspect?"

"Big-time. She can feign interest and push buttons with the best of them."

"Needless to say, this is not the sort of issue I like having dropped in my lap," she said.

"Sorry, but I thought it best to take it to you. Let's face it. On a practical level, it's a gender issue calling for a gender solution. Besides, this is my final class before graduation. I have no great interest in becoming involved in a cheating scandal."

"You are familiar with the Live Oak Community College's honor code, are you not?" she asked.

"I should be. I signed off on it," he said.

"This is the Probation Practices class, right?"

"Right."

"Today was your final?"

"Yes, but it's a two-part exam. The second comes next week."

"I'll see what I can do. I'd like to put an end to it before it becomes necessary to bring it to her father's attention, which I am more than willing to do. Cheating episodes are like wars. You can't eliminate them, so you try to minimize them. In the end, Julia must learn what it means to be a student athlete."

"Practically speaking, what does it mean?" Adam asked.

"It means you are a student first and an athlete second, and you should parcel out your time accordingly and carefully."

"Measure it out in coffee spoons."

"Yes, if necessary," she said. "Regrettably, the coaches do not always adhere to the same philosophy."

"Makes you long for your old newspaper job, no?" he asked.

"No, not at all."

"You never really explained your reason for leaving. Why did you give it up?"

She thought a moment. "You're a Shakespeare buff, Adam, but are you familiar with Milton's Paradise Lost?"

"I know he originated the word 'pandemonium' in it to help describe hell."

"Many people outside of academics are unaware of the companion poem Paradise Regained. It never received the general acclaim of the first poem. Some critics simply attribute it to the lack of action and to its brevity, but I believe the reason goes deeper and addresses a truth about people I had to confront during my years as an editor."

"Which is?" Adam interjected.

"People are more fascinated by evil than good and in the news business you are required to feed the beast. I eventually tired of it and decided to devote full time to education, hoping to steer students in directions that best suit them and society. It appears I have failed to do so with Julie, at least thus far."

She folded her arms and rocked back in her chair. "But enough of me. Is your predecessor enjoying his retirement?"

"Yes he is, though he continues to harbor a passion for the profession. He was passing through town recently and stopped in for a brief visit. It was good to see him."

"And have you found a replacement for your old position?"

"Yes. She started a short while back."

"How's she working out?"

"She's bright, but I may have put her feet to the fire too soon for someone with no experience in the field. She has an exuberance that could backfire on a dime. She's single and has lived with her grandmother for nearly her entire adult life---a sheltered life from what I gather."

"A loner. A designation usually ascribed to men," she said.

"She may see it as an opportunity to inject some excitement into her life, as many do entering the field. Sort of like the fascination with evil you were mentioning."

"Drawn like the moth to the flame, to borrow the old line."

"What I don't want to do is dampen her enthusiasm to the point of suffocating her initiative. I aim to give her free rein whenever possible."

"Like your former boss did with you," she said pointedly.

"Yes. But I need to be more discerning in handing her assignments, which brings me to my reason for being here."

"Not another cheating episode, I trust."

"No. It has to do with a current case we are working on."

Adam recounted the basics of the Murin matter from Mr. Quigley's initial account to his decision to travel to Russia. "What I'm in need of is a personal travel guide while there. Any suggestions?"

She angled her head up in thought. "Yes, as a matter of fact. Fred Jenkins in our languages department took a trip over there last year as part of an exchange program and was very complimentary about the guide assigned to their group. I don't recall the fellow's name or much else said about him, other than he was from the Ukraine."

She pulled out a desk drawer and retrieved a school directory. "I'll give you his number. You can tell him I referred you. Do you have a visa?" she asked.

"No. I have my new hire working on it."

"You can obtain one much easier and faster through the guide. I believe his company is Russian based, so he can readily generate a travel invitation from the government, which is required for a visa. They then should be able to obtain it in short order, especially if it's a tourist visa." She smiled demurely. "You did say it was partially for tour purposes, right?"

"Of course."

She paused in the middle of scribbling down the number. "This case must have grabbed you in a special way for you to go to these lengths."

"Like the bard, I'm interested in the big intrigues."

"I'd say taking on a sheriff's department detective is a big intrigue," she said.

"Snooping on cops is akin to giving a how-to speech to your peers. The audience is quickly on to your game, if you're not at the top of yours," Adam said.

"You've been giving speeches?" she asked.

"No. A fellow snoop described it as such."

"Don't you have any deadbeat dad cases to lighten the load?" she asked.

"They're on the back burner."

"You completed your course work this semester…correct?"

"Correct. As of next week I'll be finished."

"A degree in Criminal Justice to go with the English Literature one you already have. A combination you don't see often."

"A true crossing of the disciplines, encouraged and enabled by you," he said.

"Have you finally decided what you are planning to do with your degrees, Adam?"

"The same thing I'm doing now."

"Have you considered joining a government law enforcement agency? You would have greater opportunities for advancement, especially with your educational background."

"I prefer the independence a small business offers. Not only am I able to do the picking and choosing. I also get the chance to be on top of the action. Detective work in a government agency is after-the-fact. They're called in after all the action has taken place. It's the reason many cops don't seek promotion to detective level. They prefer the adrenaline rush of line duty."

"Well, here's hoping your cross disciplines can keep you free from star-crossed predicaments," she said.

"Or bail me out of them," he added.

•••

Back at the office Adam gave Fred Jenkins a ring. Yes, his instructors' group had hired a guide for their trip…a man by the name of Oleg Popov…and he turned out to be invaluable. Jenkins provided him the name of the Russian outfit Popov worked for but was unsure if he was still on board with them.

Adam turned the information over to Tamra, informing her of the visa requirements and instructing her to request it through Oleg Popov's firm. He asked her to finalize the travel arrangements by the end of the week.

"Is Mr. Quigley going to bear this added expense?" she asked.

"I'll contact him now to find out if he is willing," he said.

Adam gave Quigley a ring to inform him of his plans and to ask whether he was willing to cover the additional expense. "Yes," the ex-marine answered directly. "I can't think of anything better to spend my money on."

"I'll do my best to keep the cost to a minimum," Adam assured him. Following the call he gave the go-ahead to Tamra.

"Okay, let me first make sure I have this itinerary correct," she said in response. "You wish to fly to Moscow, meet up with the guide, preferably Oleg Popov, take the Trans-Siberian Railroad to Irkutsk and return to Moscow. However, I should leave the train and hotel arrangements to you and your guide."

"Correct."

"All in ten days' time?"

"Yes. Basically, all you have to do is arrange to get me over there and back. We'll need some flexibility within the time frame. I can't be certain how many of those days we will spend in Irkutsk. I understand it's not difficult to get same-day tickets on the Trans-Siberian. The same generally holds true with the hotels and the Russian airlines operating within the country. The one sure thing is the hiring of the guide. If you can nail him down, we can wing the rest."

"You realize this is early March and what the weather must be like where you are headed," Tamra said.

"If you're going to experience a country, what better way than in its essential raw state?"

"What should I do in case of an emergency?" she asked.

"Yours or mine?"

"Either," she said with frustration.

"For yours, call 911, if need be. If it's business related, I'll deal with it when I get back."

"And what if you need to get hold of me?"

"Consider me out of contact for two weeks…stranded in a snow bound cabin."

"With Julie Christie."

"All the more reason to leave me in complete isolation."

"What if Omar Sharif shows up?" Tamra asked.

"I'm sure he can handle rejection."

By week's end the travel arrangements were all set, including the booking of Oleg Popov as his guide. Adam was scheduled to depart Tampa the morning after his final exam. Oleg would meet him at the Moscow airport. The guide would have Adam's name scribbled on a piece of cardboard.

On his way out the door, Adam asked Tamra to try and touch base with Popov by phone to give him a heads up as to his purpose in coming, specifically to ask the guide if he would be able to gather any background information on Alex Murin, formerly of Irkutsk, Russia, prior to his arrival.

"He's a guide, not a private investigator," Tamra said.

"We all have a little detective in us waiting to get out, Tamra," he responded.

In a final flourish, Adam hit a couple of thrift stores, stocking up on temporary cold weather clothes---pullovers, khakis, boots, stocking cap, and gloves. The rushing of preparations was in keeping with his preference for spontaneity in travel. Sure, the organized tour took much of the risk out of an overseas itinerary but also the adventure. He had a mind to come and go as he pleased even if it meant chancing chaos or, yes, pandemonium.

•••

Julie Hamilton came dressed for the final in uniform, from the slit skirt down to the flip-flops. Nor did her confident demeanor differ. She obviously determined early on in the course the parameters of what she could get away with. She had sized up Professor Galenty to the point of understanding his every classroom habit, from eye movement to body placement. But for the annoying pervert Fraley ogling her legs like he was giving her a thrill or something, everything was normal. No, Galenty represented the sole threat and a minimal one at that, except it wasn't Galenty who entered the room to administer the final. It was Nancy Egan.

She walked to the front of the class, drawing quizzical gazes from students, including Adam. "I'm sure you're all wondering why I'm standing here in place of Professor Galenty. The answer is I will be serving as your proctor today in his absence," she said in a straightforward manner. "As you may know, to ensure the integrity and security of exams, the university as a matter of policy occasionally substitutes proctors for professors. Think of it in terms of a pair of fresh eyes proofreading a paper. The fresh ones spot what the tired ones don't. Not that I expect to see anything unwarranted but to be on the safe side, make sure any hats, books, notebooks, and scribbled notes are removed from desks. And while you're at it, you might as well remove the scribbled notes from body parts as well," she concluded, eliciting scattered giggles.

She proceeded to pass out the tests. Once distributed she scooted an empty chair to the head of the class, positioning it on Hamilton's side of the room, not more than four chair lengths from the leg-crosser whose knees remained locked as tight as a Victorian maiden's for the duration of the class.

Shortly before the end of class, the proctor made an announcement. "Ms. Hamilton, I'd like to see you after class. Mr. Fraley, I'd also like a moment with you before you leave."

For others in the class, totally absorbed in finishing the exam, it was nothing more than background noise, at most a passing curiosity why these two classmates were singled out for mention. For Adam it was verification of his involvement in the matter. He was unsure what his advisor had in mind but she definitely had not shelved the issue nor was she taking it lightly. As for Ms. Hamilton, she did not appear to be suffering that sinking feeling. Adam surmised she could be thinking the proctor caught the older guy Fraley in one of his ogling acts and wants to talk it over with her before she admonishes the jerk. On the other hand, there was that message she could not ignore at the beginning of class indicating a suspicion of someone cheating so perhaps she's of mind to continue on her best behavior.

Adam felt a twinge of regret for dumping the issue into his advisor's lap. Nonetheless, the school's honor code made clear a student's responsibility regarding the policing of each other. Maybe he could have handed the matter over to a dean or coach but his advisor was the one he trusted to do the right thing.

Adam completed the test and walked to the front of the classroom to place it on the instructor's desk. "I'd like to speak with you in the hallway," the proctor said in a whispered voice, whereupon he stepped outside the classroom door with her. "Are those the doctored glasses?" she asked. "Yes," he replied, "and those are the doctored legs."

A wan smile crossed her face, not the sort she had given him in prior times during happier moments. "Safe travels, Adam," she said and returned to the classroom.

He walked out of the building, his formal education at an end, his tree of knowledge yet a seedling.

CHAPTER SEVEN

The short, wiry man with the sharply drawn face awaiting him at Sheremetyevo airport wore a fur cap with earflaps, dark flannel shirt, khaki trousers belted to his lower rib cage, and weathered boots. Slung over his right arm was a wool overcoat with gloves attached to the sleeves in schoolboy style. With his left arm he was holding up a cardboard sign with Adam's name scratched on it.

The moment they made eye contact Popov casually tossed the sign into a nearby trash bin, as he undoubtedly did countless times before with arriving clients.

They shook hands. "Call me Oleg," he said congenially with barely a trace of accent.

"Adam."

"You came by way of Paris?"

"Yes, Tampa...New York...Paris...here."

"Why don't we grab your baggage then have some tea at one of these kiosks," Oleg said with a wave of the hand. "It might be best to have a preliminary meeting before we hit the ground running."

Oleg ushered him down one cavernous airport hallway after another, past large empty spaces devoid of any furnishings whatsoever. Camped on the floors were clusters of travelers in various states of repose.

Baggage in hand they trudged to the nearest kiosk for their sit-down. In the background echoed the public address system, crackling out arrival and departure times in languages for the most part indistinguishable to Adam.

"So, as I understand it," Oleg said between sips of tea, "you're mission is to gather information on a man named Alexei Murin---"

"Alex," interrupted Adam.

"Alex in English," Oleg said. "But go ahead and tell me what you have in mind."

Adam reviewed the entire case, underscoring the lack of solid evidence and his belief Murin's girlfriend in Irkutsk held the key to the case.

"For you to come this far, I take it you believe she is a co-conspirator to the crime."

"Or she is at least the motive behind the crime," Adam said.

Oleg directed his steel gray eyes at Adam. "I say this up front. I do not perform detective work. I am a travel guide who primarily offers advice on directions and locations, not people's backgrounds, unless it's an historic overview to place prominent persons in perspective."

Adam nodded his understanding, questioning the wisdom of the request he made via Tamra regarding Murin.

Oleg continued. "Having said this, I did conduct a quick background check on Murin after your office manager briefed me on you mission and was able to locate an aunt of his by the name of Darya Pronin. I have her Irkutsk address."

"A good starting point," Adam replied.

"A couple of other items I should mention," Oleg said. "The breaking up of the Soviet Union has created a buzz in this country unlike any I have experienced. It is palpable to those of us who have lived and worked here for any length of time. It will lie in the background during you entire stay. As you say with a sleeping dog, let it lie. Suspicions are running rampant, particularly in the cities. As a consequence, the general unease is likely to affect our mission."

"In what way?" Adam asked, pleased to note Oleg had said 'our' mission.

"Mother Russia is under assault from all sides. You suspect there is a Murin conspiracy. The Russian people believe there is an international conspiracy to deconstruct the Soviet Union, led by the United States. Their enmity is generally directed at American leaders, but to be on the safe side, it is probably wise for you to not wave the flag during your visit. In fact, I recommend you let me do most of the talking."

"Wouldn't want them thinking I'm a CIA operative, would we," Adam said.

"By the way, I'm not above suspicion myself," Oleg added. "I come from the Ukraine, a hotbed of secessionism."

From the main corridor arose a stir as a group of circus performers decked out in costume and acting out their roles paraded down the corridor to the amusement of passersby.

"One more item," Oleg said. "Your office manager…what's her name?"

"Tamra."

"Tamra said this was a working vacation. What exactly did you have in mind for the vacation end of it?"

"To see the Siberian countryside and people up close and personal. I figured there was no better way than by rail."

"Let me guess," Oleg said, forming his first smile. "You saw the movie Dr. Zhivago."

"Yes, I did," Adam confessed.

"Did you know it was filmed primarily in Spain? Many of the scenes were shot in summertime and paraffin was used for the snow. The actors were sweating profusely under their winter outfits."

"Please don't spoil my trip before we get started. I may have to turn around and go back," Adam quipped.

"Then you do realize what the chances are of finding Julie Christie?"

"More or less the same as finding Murin's girlfriend?"

Oleg rose from his chair. "Okay, time to go. I have reserved a cab to take us to Komsomolskya station to connect with the Trans-Siberian."

"What's the temperature reading outside?" Adam asked as they made their way to the airport exit.

"Normal for this time of the year," Oleg answered.

"Normal being what?"

"Minus five Celsius or so," came the reply. "And it could get worse where we're headed."

As if he needed a reminder he was no longer in Florida, a blast of frigid air slapped him in the face on the way out the exit. He asked himself how long had it been since he'd seen his own breath, as he puffed a lung-full of air into the Moscow atmosphere.

The taxi driver was content to keep silent during the evening rush hour drive to the station save for one instance when another driver cut him off at a busy intersection, prompting him to roll down his window and shout what Adam took to be an expletive at the offender.

"Your office manager informed me you were on a very tight budget, so we're going to start the tightening with the train trip," Oleg said from the back of the cab.

"There are three classes of rail travel…first class, which permits two persons per compartment; second class, which allows four people; and third class, called platskartny, which is essentially a dorm carriage accommodating about 50 to 60 people. We're traveling platskartny."

"I've experienced my share of dorm rooms," Adam said. "Are there any don'ts I should be aware of?"

"There's one that bears repeating: do not travel more than 15 kilometers in either direction from the tracks," Oleg said.

"Meaning what?"

"Meaning there is no right side of the tracks. Both sides are the wrong sides."

"Interesting. Are there any do's?"

"Yes, spasiba means thank you. Feel free to use it. And hang on to your American dollars. Do not exchange them, especially during this unrest. Use your credit card. Even the locals have no confidence in the ruble, which is why bartering is in such vogue."

"I have nothing to barter," Adam said, as if he should have brought bartering items along.

"Nor do I," Oleg countered, "so don't feel alone."

Adam conjured up images of historic expeditions into uncivilized territories and the necessity of explorers to have on hand objects of worth to appease the natives.

Komsomolskaya station epitomized Moscow's grandiose style. Massive chandeliers hung from lofty ceilings, spreading a soft light on the broad marble corridors below. "It's the baroque style favored by Stalin," Oleg said when he noticed Adam rubbernecking the vast interior as they made their way to the train. "Big and bold was the goal."

"As a practical matter, what are the chances of the Trans-Siberian jumping the tracks?" Adam asked.

"First thing to keep in mind is the Trans-Siberian is a route, not a train. Secondly, the safety record is generally unknown. It's like everything else in a tightly controlled society. The government broadcasts only the good events. The bad is kept under wraps. I've traveled the route numerous times and aside from a few delays and inconveniences, there were no derailments or collisions I witnessed. That's not to say accidents don't occur. Every so often rumors fly about regarding a train carrying nuclear waste leaving the tracks or a major collision occurring between a train and truck. But those are word-of-mouth reports, nothing more."

The two spoke in breathless tones as they scurried down the corridor toward their train.

"No running into cows?" Adam asked.

"When you get right down to it, there's not much to run into or over," Oleg said. "The trains travel mostly open land and the rail crossings are relatively few. The Trans-Siberian is like the government; you'd best get out of its way."

They boarded their carriage and promptly claimed two of the built-in bunk beds lining the side of the car, tossing their baggage beside and beneath the bunks. Not long after, they felt the first lurch of the train as it crept from the station and into the advancing darkness.

Squatters' rights having been determined, the two sat on the edge of their respective bunks, munching on a hodgepodge of cookies, crackers, and peanuts Adam had collected on the flights over. To wash down the snacks, Oleg dug out a couple of plastic cups and tea bags from his luggage, filling the containers with scalding hot water drawn from a stomovar located at the end of the carriage adjacent to the rest room.

"The stomovar makes carriage life bearable," Oleg said. "Without it, things could get gamy around here, since there would be no bathing, shaving, or cleaning to speak of."

"No showers?" Adam asked.

"Not in this class. You'll need to bathe by hand with the hot water. I brought along some extra soap bars and towels for you."

"What brought you from the Ukraine, Oleg," Adam mumbled through a mouthful of peanuts.

"These are tough times in the Ukraine, more so than in Russia. In short I came here for work."

"No work in the Ukraine?"

"Oh, there's work if you want to count changing light bulbs as work," Oleg said. "It may come as a surprise to you but not having a home or job is illegal under the communist system, so everyone has both, beggarly though they are."

"By homes, you mean what?"

"Bleak apartments. There are houses for the wealthier but they are in what's called the private sector. Fences surround each and every one of them. For whatever reason Russians like fences.

"Where did you learn your English?"

"At home. I'd send away for tapes of American educational programs for children on learning the basics of the language from the ABC's to Jack and Jill stuff. Sesame Street was among my favorites. Later on I enrolled in the more formal courses."

"You have a family?"

"Yes, a wife and two teenage daughters."

"Here...there?"

"There. My wife is a part-time school teacher and I'm a part-time guide working here six months out of the year."

"How long do you expect to be doing this?"

Oleg took a final swig of his tea. "This is it. My final assignment with the agency is with you. I will be returning to the Ukraine as soon as we complete the tour or the mission. I'm not sure at this point what to call it. I have managed to line up a teaching job at the same school where my wife is working, thanks to her influence."

"No travel guide openings back home?" Adam asked.

"Few, if any. There is virtually no tourism in my home country. Perhaps if we achieve our independence, the day will come when people from across the world will discover us. As it is now, the Russians want to keep us in their shadow."

"There are no significant numbers of Russians living in the Ukraine?"

"Oh, yes...large numbers...and they want to stick with the mother country," Oleg said. "Government authorities back home are sending out scanner trucks to identify citizens who are tuning in to Western television programs. The oppressive tactics are intensifying but so are the signs of change. Jeans are coming into fashion among young people. Western music can be heard everywhere. Even small private businesses are starting up."

"How has the system managed to survive this long?" Adam asked.

"For a number of reasons. You know that oft quoted line from President Kennedy: 'Ask not what your country can do for you, ask what you can do for your country.' That played very well with authorities over here. Their propaganda for the most part reflected the same sentiment. Support the system you have, they were saying. Plus, there was always the threat of military intervention in the background."

"But the system wasn't functioning," Adam said.

"Oh, it was working but not at a level to keep it competitive. Ironically, the communist economic system functions in the same manner as many western military operations. The military trains and allocates human resources according to the number of positions and vacancies available. The communists operate in a similar fashion. We need this many engineers…this many accountants…this many teachers…this many nurses to fill these numbers of positions, and so on. To do so, we will gear our educational system toward that goal. We will pick and place and you will follow."

"So where's the flaw?"

"The flaw is that the system is controlled by an ideology, not by a viable constitution. The freedom to pursue your own vocation or build your own business is severely restricted. The system stifles innovation to the degree where it is collapsing from its own inertia. It's unable to compete with the economic encroachments from the West."

"How fast is the change?"

"It's coming fast which is why high anxiety is rampant among the people. How would Americans feel if they knew for certain their government was about to collapse within days?"

"To be honest, I never thought of the Ukraine as much different from the rest of Russia," Adam said.

"At least you know there is a Ukraine," his guide responded. "We will be passing the Urals before long. They jut from Russia to the Ukraine and represent the major cultural divide between the communal ways of the East and the individualism of the West. As for the overall differences, Russia is more fast-paced and boasts a richer historical record. In the rest of the world, when one thinks of Russia, one thinks of the czars and winter. In these parts, when one thinks of the Ukraine, one thinks of potatoes and beets…breadbasket stuff. At the moment, the Ukraine is looking to reclaim its identity. Once that is seen to, we can start rewriting the text books."

"Did you always wish to be a teacher or is the government steering you into it?"

"Neither. I wanted to be a hockey player from the time I was a child."

"What happened…injury?"

"A lack of size is what happened. I was the guy who kept getting banged around the boards in the youth leagues until coaches convinced me to give the game up before I was knocked senseless."

Oleg gave Adam a sideways glance. "How about you? Detective work on your mind from the beginning?"

"No grand passion on becoming one. I sort of stumbled into it."

"But now you're engaged in a grand battle of dueling detectives."

"Never considered it in those terms."

"What is so important about it to bring you halfway around the world?"

"Getting away with murder is important…for the perpetrator, not so much for the victim."

"You mean for the family of the victim," Oleg said.

"The victim had no family, which makes it worse," Adam said. "There's no one to question or press authorities on behalf of the deceased."

"There's you," Oleg said.

"Yeah, there's me," Adam said in a deflated tone. "And here's me in Russia of all places trying to make sense of it."

Oleg stood to close a privacy curtain. "Time to get some rest," he said. "You'll have two days of sightseeing before we get back to the serious side of your business."

Adam followed in turn, closing his curtain and shedding several layers of clothing before going horizontal for the first time in a while. The warmth of the carriage came unexpectedly to him. He had braced himself for the worst, which for a Floridian meant temperatures below seventy-two degrees Fahrenheit. This was more like eighty degrees. No wonder the outside cold beckoned, a fleeting fancy if there ever was one. From his prone position, he propped his head on a hand and gazed out the window at a lone, distant light flickering in the darkness, an inkling perhaps of the mystery yet to come.

•••

Adam's bed time consisted of fits and starts, the rhythm of the rails below and the cacophony of the human activity within the carriage alternately soothing him to sleep and jarring him awake.

Daybreak brought the outside world into view, setting in motion a passing parade of power plants, factories, logging mills, and small quaint villages with colorful wooden houses, each sporting shudders to ward off the elements. But it was the endless vistas of vast landscapes carpeted by glistening snow, of ice-blue frozen rivers, of picket lines of spindly trees struggling to survive against the onslaught of wind and cold that gave the land its harsh beauty.

Adam drew aside his privacy curtain to discover people walking around in bathrobes, chatting it up with fellow travelers. A portly woman, her hair up in a bun and wearing a white smock, flitted about like a dorm mother, addressing passenger needs.

"She's called the provodnitsa...the official carriage attendant," Oleg said, catching Adam's attention to her.

It was apparent life aboard the carriage had settled into a rhythm, all aboard having carved out their space and making themselves at home.

"We have an invitation to breakfast," Oleg announced

Adam arched his eyebrows. "From who?"

Oleg angled his head over his shoulder. "From the young couple over there," he said. "They boarded in Kirov. They recognized you as an American and would like for you to regale them with tales of Florida."

"How'd they know I'm American?"

"Trust me. It's written all over you from head to foot, from the tan face, to the faded jeans, to the worn boots," Oleg answered, ticking off the tangibles in mirthful fashion.

Thereafter, while the young couple fed them delicious fresh bread and jams, along with hot tea, Adam fed them back colorful descriptions of white sand beaches and alligator infested swamps, neither of which he held a special interest in.

On the third day out of Moscow came the unexpected. Following a less fitful sleep, Adam awoke to a strange stillness. There was no clicking and clacking of wheels on railroad ties, no scraping of metal, no gentle rocking of the carriage, no movement whatsoever. They were dead on the tracks. He propped himself up on an elbow and gazed out the window to witness a still life image. Pink streaks appeared on the horizon, as the dawn's early light shimmered across an expanse of snow-packed landscape.

Inside the carriage the din of voices replaced the din of moving metal, as waking passengers scrambled about searching for answers to the train's plight.

Adam looked to Oleg's bunk where the guide sat munching on a snack. "What's the story?" he asked.

"Did you ever wonder in your wildest dreams what it would be like riding on the Trans-Siberian and having the power go out in the middle of nowhere?" Oleg asked in return.

"Can't say I have. How long have we been shut down?" he asked.

"Close to an hour," the guide answered. "Don't you notice a difference in the temperature? We're back down to normal. Of course, we will soon be far below it."

"Here's hoping we don't reach Donner Party status," Adam lamely quipped. "Any word on what went wrong?"

"There's been a lot of back and forth between the passengers and crew but no one seems to know the cause or if they do, they're not willing to reveal it. The closed society extends down to the working class level. People in charge do not readily admit failures, much less broadcast them."

"So we grin and bear it," Adam said.

"Yes, for the time being."

Adam rubbed the sleep from his eyes. "My father once told me he was riding a mail train back in the fifties from Tampa to Atlanta in the dog days of summer when the air conditioning system broke down. There was only one passenger coach and the heat became so unbearable, the train crew allowed the passengers to move into one of the mail cars. The crew slid open the doors and for the remainder of the trip they sat on mail sacks and watched the countryside fly by."

"At least you were moving," Oleg said, looking about at the milling passengers. Many were drifting in and out from other coaches in search of answers. By default, they all had become members of a classless society.

"This thing's electrically powered...right?" Adam asked, having noted the power lines running above the tracks.

"Yes. On some sections of the route they still utilize diesel trains but we're on an electrical stretch here."

"Any hot water left in the stomovar?"

Oleg reached under his bunk and pulled out a jug. "It's cold water now," he said, handing the container over.

Adam scrounged for a packet of peanuts and a few cookies and indulged in a makeshift breakfast. "What chance is there of another train coming to our aid?' he asked.

"I have no idea," Oleg answered. "It all depends on what the problem is. "Perhaps there was a wreck ahead, perhaps a part of the tracks are damaged, perhaps the engineer collapsed and died. It's all speculation at this point. I assume it's an electrical issue of some sort. There has been no westbound traffic since we stalled, which leads me to believe the problem is system-wide."

"The entire route shut down?" Adam asked incredulously.

"More likely it's limited to a section of it. The fact is we will probably never know."

The temperature in the carriage continued to dip. Passengers were adding layers of clothing by the minute. Through windows covered with grime, Adam noticed a goodly number of passengers had exited the train, opting for the frigid clean air over the acrid atmosphere building within the carriage. Those remaining were becoming increasingly cranky, grumbling to each other while walking around with the usual scowls on their faces.

Adam's gaze drifted from the trackside to the bordering landscape. Approximately a quarter of a mile away atop a slope stood a bright blue and green cottage with a corrugated metal roof, partly obscured by several stands of birch trees. He pointed the small house out to Oleg. "Whenever I traveled cross country with my parents by train and we would pass these isolated homes in mostly uninhabitable territory, I would always wonder who lived there, why they lived there, and what did they do for a living. If I had had the choice, I would have stopped the train to walk up and knock on their door to find out what circumstances in life led them there."

Oleg followed Adam's gaze out the window. "Well, if ever the opportunity presented itself, it's now."

"You serious?" Adam asked, surprised at his guide's suggestion.

"Why not? There might be a hot cup of tea in store for us, or something even more enticing…something long dwelling in that imagination of yours."

They hurriedly donned extra layers of clothing, threaded their way through mingling passengers to the rear of the carriage, and hopped down the exit ramp to the track bed and into freezing temperatures. To their favor the wind was nearly non-existent, making it by Siberian standards a mild day.

Adam gauged the distance between the track bed and the house on the hill. "Looks to be a twenty minute hike up the hill and back," he said. "Figure a ten minute visit; that gives us a half hour total. How soon do you think they'll get this thing rolling?"

Oleg tied the flaps of his hat under his chin. "I have no idea but keep in mind they wouldn't have let the passengers off, if they thought it would be a brief delay. Secondly, the train will not be out of our sight, so we will know when re-boarding is taking place. Thirdly…" Oleg paused to look up and down the tracks. "What's the third thing?" Adam asked impatiently. "The third thing to keep in mind is that they won't hesitate to leave without us," his guide answered, pulling on his gloves.

"Let's do it," Adam said, fidgeting like a restless thoroughbred ready to bolt.

The two bounded from the track bed to the snow packed turf. As soon as they took off, the provodnitsa shouted something out to them.

"What'd she say?" Adam asked.

"'Don't go far' with an expletive thrown in," Oleg said.

The conversation was muted as the two adventurers huffed and puffed their way up the hillside to the first line of skinny birch trees standing two hundred meters above the track bed. A cold sun had broken through a thin layer of clouds to add a luster to the paper-like black and white bark of the barren trees.

Adam turned to glance back down the slope. Passengers continued to mill about outside the train. Looking back up the slope, he could make out the house beckoning beyond the trees.

They were passing through the outer edge of woods when a loud pop pierced the quiet, halting them in their tracks. Adam cupped his hands over his eyes and squinted into the fierce morning sunlight. "Was that what I think it was?" he asked, exchanging glances with Oleg. He shaded his eyes for a second look. Through the glare appeared a shadowy figure partially hidden by a tree. Was that a rifle in his hands? A second pop confirmed his suspicion, as a piece of bark snapped from the trunk of a close-by birch. He looked every which way trying to decipher from what direction the shots were coming. A third kicked a puff of snow up several feet in front of them. In the same instant, the train's whistle sounded, signaling for the passengers to get back aboard.

Oleg looked up and down the hillside before turning to face Adam. "We can either get shot or be left here to freeze to death. I suggest we beat a retreat."

"Excellent idea," Adam said.

The pair stumbled and slipped down the hill in lung-burning haste. When they were fifty meters from the track bed only a handful of passengers remained to board. At twenty meters all were aboard except for the two hill climbers. A member of the train crew had yet to raise the boarding ramp, perhaps taking pity on the two stumbling toward them.

Adam turned to urge his trailing companion on. Oleg's cheeks were puffing in and out with the elasticity of a trumpet player's, but he persevered. The moment Adam set foot on the ramp the train lurched ahead. He grabbed the handrail and reached with his free hand for Oleg. Clasping his wrist he hauled him aboard. Catching their breath on the landing, they thanked the crewman who proceeded to give them a dressing down.

Soon thereafter the carriage atmosphere was back to normal, giving both men the chance to rehash their experience.

"The guy probably thought the entire train would end up at his doorstep," Adam concluded. "I figure he was trying to scare us off."

"Or a bad shot," Oleg said. "And who says it was a man? It could have been the lady of the house."

"Or a hunting cabin, with the hunter mistaking us for bears," Adam said.

"Bears, if there're out of hibernation, don't hang out this close to the tracks in the daytime," Oleg countered. "They don't care to be seen. They wait till night to prowl for scraps thrown by crewmen."

For the remainder of the day, Adam listened as Oleg traded stories and food with clusters of passengers anxious to display their hospitality. "They are mostly people who use the Trans-Siberian as a commuter train between settlements," Oleg explained at the end of one group get-together. "You'll find few tourists aboard the Trans-Siberian other than the occasional backpacker."

On scheduled stops Adam and his guide exited the train to partake of the abundance of foods offered by the platform vendors. At each stop old women dressed in smocks and scarves, their embroidered aprons billowing in the wind, scampered from out of nowhere to hurriedly to set up tables and display their foods. Among the passenger favorites were milk, sour milk, homemade cheeses, ice cream, chicken, baked potatoes, and smoked fish. All the while, the distinct odors of coal, smoke, coffee, garlic, sausage, and the ever-present vodka wafted across the platforms.

"One thing about the food breaks," Oleg said with a wink. "The trains run on time. They will leave without you. So it's best to keep abreast of the time."

"I'll leave that up to you," Adam said. "I'm already lost when it comes to the time of day."

By mid-morning of the fourth day, they were less than an hour out of Irkutsk according to Oleg. "The town is on the opposite side of the Angara River from the station," the guide said. "However, there is a bridge and a regular tram service connecting the two. Also, in keeping with our budget conscious travel, there is a very inexpensive hostel style accommodation offered in the station. It's another dorm style arrangement located on the opposite end of the main corridor. Think you can handle it?"

"Fine with me," Adam replied. "What is that standard clause in divorce suits…in the style of living I've grown accustomed to? That's me at this stage."

They had time for a final meal of bread, fruits, and tea prior to arrival. Through the din of carriage chatter came the squeal of wheels scraping the rails as the train rounded a sharp curve and headed for the station.

Adam was one leg closer to discovering if he had journeyed halfway around the world for nothing.

CHAPTER EIGHT

Tamra picked through the day's mail, entertaining the notion of her boss finding the time to send a postcard, anything to break the boredom of holding down the fort. Fielding phone messages and deferring the inquiries of present and potential clients until his return was an exercise in tedium. Yes, it was part of the learning process but it was light years removed in terms of excitement from the jousting with Alex Murin, a high she had yet to come down from. Yet, in the midst of the monotony, the excitement returned the moment she arrived back from a brief work break to see detective Murin standing in front of her desk as if he'd been dropped from the clouds.

For the previous encounters, she had been prepared. For this one she felt like the fort was suddenly under siege and she its ill-equipped defender.

A rush of questions crowded her mind as she approached him. Why was he here? To see her boss? To see her? If so, how did he know she worked here? Did he recognize her from the bar? From the house caper? Does he know about the investigation?

"Hello Tamra," he said in gentleman-like fashion.

"Hello…Alex was it?"

"Yes. Can we talk?"

She motioned to the chair fronting her desk. "What brings you here?"

"You," he said up front.

"Oh…okay," she said. "How did you know I worked here?"

"One of the guys who was at Orologio's the night we met tipped me he had seen you coming in and out of here on several occasions, so I dropped in to see if, in fact, it was you."

Tamra folded her hands on the desk. "Well then, what can I do for you?" she asked, attempting a formal tone.

A coy smile slowly creased his face. "It's a social visit," he said.

He may be a murder suspect, Tamra thought, making light of the notion, but God was he handsome, something she wanted to say to Adam but didn't the moment her boss first flashed Murin's photo to her. And now the guy struts in looking gorgeous, wearing a powder blue shirt, form-fitting jeans, with a confident face framed by styled, shaggy blond hair. It was as though one of those Russian male ballet dancers with the muscled limbs and rhythmic motions had bounded off the television screen and into her life.

"First, let me apologize for some of my remarks at Orologio's. They were out of line," he said. "Like I said, I'm known for saying what others are thinking."

Tamra flicked her hand in a dismissive gesture. "No need. I've heard much worse."

Murin glanced at his watch. "Then I'll jump to my second reason for stopping by. I'd like a second chance with you at Orologio's. How about lunch?"

She turned and glanced at a wall clock across the room. Like many single women, she held in reserve readily available rejection lines for just such occasions, the sort to ease hurt feelings.

She summoned a smile. "I'm all for second chances," she said.

Whether her boss would approve or not was a moot point. She was the person in charge at the moment. And wasn't it Adam who early on taught her by example the value of reasonable risk? The reality was he was on the other side of the world in search of something she could by chance uncover

over lunch. "Go for it!" she could hear him say from half a world away.

•••

Orologio's at lunch hour was a shell of itself. Gone were the cramped aisles and raised voices, replaced by roomy corridors and quiet conversation. At Murin's request the hostess led them to an isolated corner table for two.

"Here's to the gumshoe trade," Murin said, as they clinked wine glasses. "Your boss off on assignment?"

"He's off on vacation," she said, leaving it there.

"What sort of detective work is he involved in?"

"The usual...cheating spouses...background checks...runaway kids. What about you?"

"The usual...murder...attempted murder...robbery...drug busts...so on."

"Your usual sounds more weighty than our usual," she said.

Murin shook his head. "All are weighty to the parties involved. The cases may differ but the fundamental procedures are similar. The goal for the investigator is to gather evidence to decide whether a case is to be made or not...solid evidence, that is, not the skimpy kind. This may sound odd coming from a cop but I view a false accusation as heinous as the crime allegedly committed. If you really want to balance the scales of justice, the penalty for lodging a bogus charge should equal the penalty for the alleged crime. Unfortunately, the false accusations in too many instances are enough to ruin reputations." The detective angled his head and looked at her inquisitively. "Have you ever had a family member, friend, or acquaintance falsely charged, Tamra?"

She nodded. "Yes, the husband of a friend of mine. He was a high school teacher. He was falsely accused of inappropriate conduct toward a female student. And you are right. The accusation itself was enough to get him suspended while the investigation was carried out. Ultimately, he was found innocent of the charge but the mark remained in the eyes of many in the community. It nearly tore the family apart."

97

"Those sorts of cases are especially ripe for false charges," Murin said. "Look at all the recent daycare child abuse accusations that were thrown about. If you were a male working in a childcare center, you were presumed to be guilty. And how many of those charges turned out to be true? Very few of them were, if any. The collateral damage was monumental. It was like a contagion."

"And in the teacher's case, his accuser was given a slap on the wrist," Tamra said, finding herself in agreement.

"On the plus side, the false accusations are taken more seriously by the courts than they are by the press," Murin said. "Perjury charges are frequently filed by prosecutors, but often these are buried on the inside pages."

The detective folded his arms on the table and leaned forward in a time-to-change-the-subject gesture. "Am I out of line in saying you're looking terrific today?"

"No," she said politely. "Thank you."

"I have to ask…what were you doing here all alone last week?"

"Waiting on a friend. Unfortunately, we had a mix-up in schedules," she said without a blink of the eye.

Murin leaned back. "A prospective employer once asked me to provide him my life story in a paragraph. Not that you asked, but here it is. Born and raised in Irkutsk, Russia, attended post-secondary school in Omsk, returned to Irkutsk to work in the security business, migrated to this country to pursue greater opportunities, married an American girl and subsequently went to work for the sheriff's department."

She raised her eyebrows. "You're married?"

"No longer. My wife was killed in an auto accident a while back."

Tamra furrowed her brow. "I'm terribly sorry."

A brief silence ensued, broken by a waiter delivering their meals, hers a Caesar's salad, his a grouper sandwich.

"Your turn," he said.

She hesitated to collect her thoughts. "Okay, my life in a paragraph. Born and raised in Altoona, Pennsylvania, moved to Tampa following high school to strike out on my own, ended up living with my grandmother who retired here years ago, worked as a secretary for two different companies before taking my present position." She paused. "Makes life seem simple minus all the details, doesn't it?"

"I take it you never married," Murin said. "Makes me want to ask what's wrong with the Tampa Bay guys. No chemical reactions thus far?"

"My grandmother is always telling me, 'remember, if it's love you're looking for, it's love that will find you.' Furthermore, I don't believe in chemistry." At least until now, she thought.

"Why so?"

"Chemistry between people is a transitory thing. You have to look beyond it. I prefer the enduring traits...trust, honesty, loyalty, and so on."

"You take the long-term view," Murin noted.

"Yes. You go around and ask longtime married couples what's the secret to the longevity of their marriage and seldom do they cite chemistry as the reason."

"But who's talking marriage," Murin countered. "Enjoy the moment, I say." He raised his wine glass. "Do keep listening to your grandmother, though. She sounds like a wise woman."

"Oh, I'll definitely keep listening to her. It's too bad age is a requirement for wisdom. It's the one value this world is lacking most in my opinion."

"Agreed," Murin said.

"I worry about her though. She spends most of the day alone while I'm at work. It's become more worrisome because of all the break-ins occurring in our neighborhood recently."

"What section of town do you live in?" he asked

"The Edgewood district."

"There's a way of relieving your anxiety, Tamra. Both the sheriff's department and the city police keep hotspot checklists. They will patrol an area daily to curb a sharp hike in crime activity. I can see to it Edgewood is added to the list if it is not already on there."

"That is very considerate," she said. "I know how difficult the allocation of personnel can be when you're working with limited resources."

Murin locked his eyes on hers. "Tamra, let me throw a proposal at you. The department is making a big effort to add more women to the force. How about you joining up with us? The pay and benefits are good, probably much better than what you are receiving now. Your brief experience with your current job will count for something, plus I can put in a good word for you...good enough to get you on board, I'm sure."

Taken by surprise, Tamra's immediate reaction was to downplay the idea. "I'm not sure I have the qualifications. My short time at the detective agency hardly qualifies me."

Murin pressed on. "There's a written test, physical test, psychological test, and an interview, all of which you would pass with ease."

"What about the formal education requirements?"

"All that is required is a high school diploma or GED."

She pondered the idea. "At one time I considered joining the military, but it would have required me to leave home, which I am unable to do because of my grandmother. I couldn't leave her."

"All the more reason to join us," he said with eagerness. "You wouldn't have to leave home. And once you came on board, the advancement opportunities are there for the taking. All sorts of specialized fields are opening from forensics to public relations. It's a chance to start a career, not be stuck in a dead end job. Nothing against your present position, but there is no comparison when it comes to advancement."

She took a bite of her salad and struck a thoughtful pose. "I'll consider it," she said.

Murin pressed no further, letting the proposal stand. "Good," he said and headed in a different direction. "Do you know what the name Tamra means in Russian?" he asked.

"No. Something frigid, I suppose," she said.

He chuckled, deepening his dimples. "On the contrary, someone in your past must have divined that Florida was in your future. It means palm tree."

She gave him a hard look. "Seriously, I doubt my parents had that in mind. Besides, few people I'm aware of associate palm trees with Russia."

"Not like one can associate Tamra with palm trees," he said. Curiosity crossed her face.

"Let me count the ways," he said. "Both are tall, both exotic, both sultry, and both bend but don't break."

"Speculating with the last one, are you not?"

"I have a gift for speculation, backed up by keen observation of course."

"Since we're playing what's in a name, how about Alexei, or Alex as you prefer?"

"Actually, it's from the Greek. It means defender."

"Of the country…of the family…of the faith?" She asked.

"All of the above, I'd like to think," he said and proceeded to elaborate on the confusion caused by Russian names, how a single person can be called by many names, how important it is to address the person by his first name followed by the middle name, which is taken from the first name of the father."

"I'll keep it in mind the next time I tackle a Russian novel," she said. "I seem to lose track of the characters in the jumble of first names, middle names, family names, and nicknames."

"So you do read books after all," Murin said, reminding her of their previous repartee at the bar.

"Don't look so shocked. I have a library card, you know," she said in a teasing tone. "I read Brothers Karamazov and until I got the hang of it halfway through, I had great difficulty separating the characters."

"Who was your favorite brother?" he asked in earnest.

She smiled coyly. "Alyosha, of course, the kind and gentle one. And you?"

"Dmitri Fyodorovich Karamazov," he answered promptly. "Dmitri understood the weakness of human flesh---which is to be celebrated on special occasions." He lifted his wine glass to take a sip, as though toasting the thought.

She offered not a word in return. Instead, she picked up from the table a small promotional card highlighting the dessert menu, eliciting the response she expected.

"Would you care for dessert?" he asked.

Tamra continued to peruse the menu, ostensibly debating the question. "I think I'll pass, though I must confess cheesecake is one of my guilty pleasures," she said, turning the card toward him. "Are you a cheesecake lover?"

Murin ignored the card, zeroing his eyes in on her. "I can live without cheesecake," he said, "though my deceased wife had an incurable craving for it."

He drove her back to the office, the conversation along the way devoted to comparisons of English and Russian writers, Tamra asking at one point if there was a Russian female equivalent of Flannery O'Connor. "Who's Flannery O'Connor?" he asked in response.

"May I see you again?" he asked on arrival.

She smiled and let the question go unanswered. "I seem to recall you have a lady friend back home you are engaged to in one way or the other," she purposely said.

"What's an engagement, Tamra, other than a test of a relationship?" he said in his parting words to her.

Alex Murin occupied her mind for the remainder of the day. He was a hard one to figure, she deduced, recalling what her grandmother had to say about women and their great skill in judging the character of other women, yet at the same time how unskilled they were in judging men.

What did she take from the get-together? One, it was not an unmarked sheriff's car he was driving today, as insignificant as that might be. Two, he was not the one who craved cheesecake, so he said. Three, he had an interest in her, carnal though it might be. Four, unless more solid evidence surfaced branding him a definite suspect, she would continue to entertain an interest in him.

Oblivious to the clock, the afternoon flew by as swiftly as her thoughts. At last, weary from contemplation, she closed shop, concluding there was nothing like a little sexual tension to speed up the workday.

CHAPTER NINE

Their dorm space staked out and settled into, Adam and his guide walked to an unoccupied station waiting room to map out their strategy for the day.

"The aunt's name is Darya Pronin," Oleg said. "She lives alone in an apartment complex on Dzerzhinsky Street near the center of the city right across from where we sit."

"Is it within walking distance?" Adam asked.

"Yes." Oleg checked his watch. "I told her we would be there in a half hour."

"How did you manage to locate the aunt in the first place?"

"I didn't. I have to credit our home office for the find. They receive many requests from tourists regarding long lost relatives. They're thinking we may be able to hook them up. As a consequence, the office set up a sub unit to handle the requests. It is low-funded and low-manned...definitely a hit-and-miss operation when it comes to results. Somehow, they came up with a hit on this one. I suspect they worked the phones, which is normally the extent of their effort."

"I'm convinced Murin's girlfriend holds the key to unraveling this thing," Adam said. "Though the aunt will be a good starting point. We'll need to pump her for as much background information as we can. First, though, we need to find out if she's kept in contact with Murin. If so, there's the chance she may have tipped him off to our coming."

"What exactly is it you're looking for?" Oleg asked.

"Hard evidence."

"Like?"

"Like a piece of correspondence. Needless to say, the two had to be corresponding. Murin knows the safest method is by mail. Authorities here and in the States are easily able to monitor calls...right?

"Here for sure...anything else you're looking for?" Oleg asked.

"There's always the chance we could stumble across someone who could corroborate what we suspect. Depends on where our search leads us." Adam stood and yanked on his stocking cap. "Let's get to it."

"Before we get started, there's something I should tell you," Oleg said, stifling a smile.

"What is it?"

"Irkutsk is often referred to as the Paris of Siberia."

"Which means little to me, since I've never set foot there," Adam responded.

"You're forgetting your Paris layover," Oleg pointed out.

"Airports don't count. They are like independent territories."

"You say that as if it's settled law."

"Settled in my mind."

Beneath a leaden sky and with a biting wind at their back, they set out on their trek, taking the tram across the Angara River to downtown Irkutsk. Adam followed on Oleg's heels as they strode down walkways bordering broad streets and busy intersections manned by bundled up cops directing traffic. To Adam it was surprising to see a relatively modern urban city planted in the middle of Southern Siberia. So much for preconceptions, he thought. He noted how schizophrenic the city appeared in its architecture. Buildings designed like wedding cakes, pipe organs and curled ice cream cones, many colored in salmon and turquoise hues, alternated with drab, concrete structures resembling public housing back in the States. Juxtaposition of opposites seemed to be the theme.

Upon reaching Dzerzhinsky Street, Oleg plucked a slip of paper from his back pocket to check the street number. "This way," he said, pointing down the avenue. Further on they went into a flower shop at Oleg's suggestion to purchase a bouquet for Darya. "A Russian custom when visiting," the guide explained. Five minutes later they approached one of the block concrete structures, an apartment complex of considerable size. Entering a sterile gray lobby, Adam sighted an elevator off to the side. "What floor is she on?" he asked, slapping the cold from his arms.

"The fourth."

Adam pointed in the direction of a stairwell adjacent to the elevator. "Let's climb it."

"Why?"

"I need the exercise."

"After we trudged a mile to get here?" Oleg said, trailing after him. "By the way, it is a Russian tradition for visitors to remove their shoes before entering a home."

"I like it," Adam said. "My toes need wiggling."

Arriving on the fourth floor, Oleg handed the flowers to Adam and checked his notes again. Continuing on, they walked past a line of apartment doors, eventually stopping to knock on one. An instant later the door swung open. Filling the doorway was a woman wearing a floor length red smock and a blond wig fifty years younger than her chubby face. Adam figured her a onetime gold medalist in the women's shot put for the Soviet Union national track and field team.

Adam handed Darya the flowers, as she stepped back and invited them in with a sweep of the hand. The two visitors removed their shoes as greetings flew back and forth between Darya and Oleg, both acting like long lost kin.

The visitors took seats on a large couch upholstered in the same garish floral pattern as two companion armchairs across the room. Above the chairs a series of Russian Orthodox icons adorned pink walls. In a corner stood a vintage television set Adam was convinced would display a black and white test pattern if switched on.

Darya moved to a tiny kitchen situated side by side with a bathroom. A smile continually played across her face as she engaged in animated conversation with Oleg in Russian. Lining the kitchen walls were shelves filled with ornamental jugs and jars containing a variety of spices and herbs. In short order, she returned with hot tea, fresh bread, berry jam, and butter.

"She says she knew Murin quite well when he was very young," Oleg said, filling him in on the conversation. "She sometimes baby sat him. However, she lost track of him when the family moved to Omsk. As far as she knows, he attended both high school and college there."

"Ask her, when was the last time she saw him," Adam said, separating a chunk of the warm bread.

Oleg repeated the question to Darya who answered without hesitation. He then turned to Adam. "This qualifies as interesting. She ran into him at a restaurant here in Irkutsk several years ago before he moved to America---"

"How'd she know he moved to America?" Adam interrupted.

"I informed her over the phone when I set this meeting up. Anyway, to continue, Murin told her he was here to visit a woman by the name of Alina Novikov. Alina was his childhood sweetheart. She says he adored her."

"That was the last time she spoke to him?"

"Yes."

"Does she know how long their relationship lasted?"

With each question Darya would peer over her teacup at Adam and then dart her eyes to Oleg as he repeated the question.

"She doesn't know. As she mentioned, once the families drifted apart, she lost contact."

"So she never saw Murin and Alina again?"

Oleg relayed the question to Darya. In the middle of her lengthy response, Oleg slowly lifted a forefinger to Adam indicating there may be something significant forthcoming.

"What is it?" Adam asked before she had finished her answer.

The translator waited till she concluded. "She recalls a story in the local paper a year or so ago about a cultural exchange mission to America. The mission represented all segments of Russian society from government officials to ordinary citizens. There were photos of the mission members. Alina was among them. Want to guess where the mission was headed to?"

"Where?"

"Your home town of Tampa."

"She sure it was Tampa?" Adam eagerly asked.

"Yes. I asked her the same question. She's positive because an uncle of hers migrated there before moving to New York. He was constantly complaining of the heat and mosquitoes."

On hearing Oleg's translation, Darya at once pointed a finger at Adam and commenced slapping her arms and face in manic fashion, laughing uproariously as she did so.

"She wants to know if that's what you do all day back home," Oleg said.

Adam, in turn, immediately abandoned his reserve, leaping from his seat to mimic her actions by flailing his arms and hands about like a crazed animal under assault from a swarm of the pests. His antics caused Darya to nearly double over in raucous laughter.

Meanwhile, Oleg set back and casually finished off his tea and bread while waiting for the hilarity to subside.

Ending his act, Adam resumed questioning. "Does Alina still live here?" he asked.

Oleg passed the question along to Darya who quickly rose from her chair and walked to the kitchen to retrieve a phone book and hand it to Oleg. The guide fingered through pages till he settled on an entry. "Here's an A. Novikow," he said, taking out a slip of paper from his pocket and jotting down the address.

"Does she know the location of the address?"

Oleg read it off to her. "Nyet," she said and followed with a question of her own.

"She wants to know if we are on a mission," Oleg said.

"Da," Adam said, the da sounding like duh.

She nodded her head as though she understood.

Oleg stood to signal it was time to leave. "Spasiba," he said, extending a hand. She took it and Adam's also. "Spasiba," she said with vigor. "Spasiba."

They donned their shoes and left. Content with their findings, they returned to the rail station waiting room to map out their strategy.

"Okay, here's what we know," Adam said. "Correct me if I'm wrong. Alina and Murin were childhood sweethearts. Because of family disruptions, the two became separated at a young age for a lengthy period of their lives. Years later, for whatever reason, Murin returns to Irkutsk to look Alina up...probably to resurrect the relationship. We are not sure if, in fact, they hooked up or not. He later moves to America to start a new life. A year ago she's part of a cultural exchange mission to Tampa. Sound right?"

"The sequence sounds right. The question is what do you make of it?"

"I'm betting they reconnected in Tampa during the cultural exchange event."

"Which fueled what followed," Oleg said. "Now what?"

"It's time for some good old surveillance," Adam said. "Let's go see what Alina is up to."

•••

Adam and his guide agreed to forego their economy travel and spring for a rental car. They needed speed and flexibility of movement. A bus or a taxi offered neither. Furthermore, there was a rental car agency conveniently located right around the corner from the rail station.

Oleg chose a pea green Ladel for them to rent. "A nice little car...handles well in the snow," he said. They also picked up an

Irkutsk street map to guide them. Adam, they decided, would do the driving and Oleg the navigating.

According to the map, Alina lived in a residential district close to the eastern edge of the city. Street signs installed on tops of bus stations helped direct them. A half hour out of downtown they were on a narrow tree-lined street where Alina lived. Adam slowed the car to a crawl to allow Oleg to monitor the house numbers.

"It must be near the far end of the street," his guide advised, motioning ahead.

Restrictions on the shapes and sizes of houses must be non-existent, Adam observed, though nearly all were wooden with the usual brightly colored shudders attached.

Adam realized they were on a dead-end street the instant he spotted a thickly wooded area ahead.

Oleg checked the address he had scribbled on the map. "It should be the last house on the right," he said.

Coming into view was a cottage-sized abode nestled against a wall of towering spruce trees. Directly across the street from the Novikov home was a house with what appeared to be a wooden cross rising from its rooftop. To the rear of the house was a small cemetery bordered by a picket fence. Mounted above each gravesite was a tiny wooden shrine housing religious icons.

"Why don't you pull into that church house's parking lot," Oleg suggested.

"What's a church house?"

"They're independent churches. Families or neighbors band together to convert houses into churches as an alternative to the orthodox parish churches. The Soviet government began banning them years ago but many continue to function."

"Any chance services are about to begin?"

"There's always a chance though it appears from the inactivity this is not a likely day or time."

Adam turned into the church's empty parking lot, swinging the car to a stop at an angle, which allowed them a full view of Alina's residence.

They sat in silence for a minute, assessing the lay of the land and the cottage across the way. In its driveway was parked a Ladel, no less, of deep blue color. For the first time since they arrived in Irkutsk, light snow flurries filled the sky, dancing up and down on their way to the ground.

"Now the real work starts," Adam said, switching off the engine.

"What work?" Oleg asked.

"Sitting on your ass and doing nothing until the quarry makes a move. It could be in five minutes or five hours."

"We're not even sure it's the right Novikov," Oleg said.

"Part of the elimination process," Adam replied.

Oleg leaned back and rested his head on the seat. "This your most unusual case, Adam?"

He thought a moment. "Unusual? No, I wouldn't call it unusual…here's unusual," he said, dialing back the past. "I once got a request from an attorney living in a neighboring county in Central Florida to assist him in a case that was about to go to court. His client held the position of Tax Collector for the county. His name was Harold Gantt. He was relatively new on the job but in the short time he was there, he earned a reputation as a solid and well-respected manager. I can vouch for this because I was the one who conducted the background check on him at the request of his attorney. The guy was as pure as this snow," Adam said, nodding to the flakes playing touch and go on the car windshield.

"So, what was the problem?" Oleg asked

"The problem started when somebody in the county government came up with the bright idea of having a 'Bail-Your-Boss-Out-of-Jail' day. The gist of it was that employees could nominate their boss to be 'arrested' on the job and taken to jail where he or she would sit until bailed out by their employees, the 'bail' money going to charity. Unbeknownst to

112

Mr. Gantt, he was nominated by his staff. It should be noted much of the general public not to mention a good portion of the county staff were unaware of the promotion, including Gantt. The game was mainly reserved for the higher-ups who were targeted in order to get the biggest return---a county manager, an assistant county manager, a personnel director, a sheriff, and the like. Well, when the 'Bail-Your-Boss-Out-of-Jail' day arrived, Mr. Gantt was in his office as usual, diligently working on his assignments while his employees, some forty or fifty of them, sat expectantly at their desks waiting for the show to start. They didn't have to wait long. About an hour after opening, two sheriff's deputies stepped through the front door, stalked past the rows of desks, and disappeared into Gantt's office. A few minutes later, a ruckus could be heard from inside his office. The next thing you know, one deputy came stumbling out with Mr. Gantt riding on his back, as the other deputy struggled to clamp the cuffs on Gantt. Eventually, they got him under control and marched him out the door."

"What happened?" Oleg asked. "Was it all part of the act?"

"That's what the staff was thinking at the time. But it wasn't part of an act. Like I said, Gantt had a clean record. Turns out, he also was a prideful man and had a short fuse, which the record did not indicate. He knew there was no reason for him to be arrested and he took great offense, physically resisting their efforts to cuff him."

"Didn't the deputies explain their reason for being there?"

"Apparently explaining why they were there to arrest him was not part of the act. Consequently, things escalated quickly and the deputies ended up hauling the tax collector out the door. One of the deputies received a bruise from the scuffle."

"They actually charged him?"

"There's the rub. They couldn't charge him with resisting arrest since, in reality, they weren't there to arrest him. Nor could they charge him with assault because, like his attorney said, he was acting in self-defense. After all, the deputies made the first move---the first laying on of hands."

"You said they were about to go to court. What did they end up charging him with?" Oleg asked.

"Would you believe disorderly conduct?'

Oleg shook his head. "You serious?"

"Yes, but finally cooler heads prevailed, and all the parties involved realized how foolish they looked and the charge was dropped. Mr. Gantt returned to work with his spotless record intact. To nobody's surprise the county commissioners officially scrapped 'Bail-Your-Boss-Out-of-Jail' day."

"And that's my stakeout story for the day," Adam concluded. "How about you? This your most unusual assignment?"

"One of a kind," his guide responded.

"Beyond the call of duty?"

"Probably so, but I need a good story to go out on…one to tell my grandchildren."

Adam reached over to punch on the car radio and scan the stations, only to find every other one blaring some variation of martial music.

"Very patriotic nation nowadays," Oleg commented.

Adam finally landed on one with people engaged in conversation.

"Talk radio," Oleg said, following a minute of listening.

"Talking about what?"

"America."

"Lots of nice talk, right?"

"Think of talk radio in the United States and what people have to say about the Soviet Union and then reverse the countries and that's what you have here."

Adam pressed the radio off.

"What convinces you this client of yours is correct in his conjecturing for you to go to all this trouble?" Oleg asked, breaking a brief silence.

"I believe him," Adam answered firmly. "Isn't that what all life boils down to…who do you believe in? Plus, I like to level

114

the playing field and this field is as unbalanced as a crooked cop's mind."

The snow flurries continued over the next hour, dusting the empty street. At regular intervals Adam started the engine to warm the car and to clear the windshields with a couple of swipes of the wipers.

"How old would you say that chimney of hers is?" Adam asked.

"It's an old one," Oleg replied. "Exactly how old, I have no idea."

"In the states the old ones are close to eighteen inches in diameter."

"These may be a bit broader...why, do you have something in mind?"

"The crown on the new ones back home prevent entry by people or animals," Adam continued. "You know anything about the crowns here?"

"I know they are not elaborate. Oftentimes, people will simply fit a piece of mesh to the flue and replace it periodically."

"Not a sound safety measure," Adam said. "What's to prevent an intruder from dropping down?"

"That's what the Glock is for," Oleg quipped. "Furthermore, most intruders would find another way in."

"If I'm not mistaken, those little windows of hers look to be sealed tight," Adam observed.

"Sealed securely more to prevent the cold from entering than intruders," Oleg said. "An intruder could always bust open a window."

"A wily intruder might want to leave everything intact to make it appear there was no intrusion," Adam said. "Remind me to get some rope."

"Would not this be evidence illegally obtained," Oleg asked, "if there is any to be obtained in the first place?"

"In the States it might, but when it's evidence obtained overseas, it becomes complicated, especially if it's obtained by a third party."

"Who might the third party be?"

Adam grinned.

"I repeat. I'm solely a guide. I'm stretching the job description as is," Oleg said.

"And I'm claustrophobic," Adam retorted. "Remember, I'm the guy who won't ride elevators."

"We can decide later," Oleg said. "Right now I'm concerned we're beginning to stick out like a sore thumb, sitting here all alone for this length of time."

Not a single car had appeared on the scene. Not totally unexpected, since they were parked at the end of a dead end street.

Oleg spread the map across his lap. "We're here," he said, pointing to their present location. "In case the authorities come checking, we're supposed to be here," he said, fingering a spot not too far distant. "Our story is we're sitting here trying to figure out how to get from here to there. I---"

Oleg's response was cut short by a hand gripping his shoulder. A movement at the front entrance of the cottage had caught Adam's eye. In the next instant the door opened wide and into their lives stepped Alina Novikov. "It's her," Adam said, absorbing the moment. "Is it any wonder they sent her on the cultural exchange mission?"

Oleg refolded the map. "How can you be sure?" he asked.

"I'm sure."

A slender woman, she wore a long black leather overcoat, fur boots, and a fur hat capping wavy blond locks. She brushed the dusting of snow from her windshield with a gloved hand and slid into the car.

"What time is it?" he asked Oleg.

"Close to four. She's headed for work, it's safe to say."

Adam started the engine and pulled out onto the street, trailing her at a discreet distance.

The path she traveled led them back to the central city in the vicinity of the rail station. Ultimately, she turned into a narrow alleyway leading to the rear of a place Oleg translated as "The Caviar Café." Adam circled the block to give her time to enter the restaurant.

"Her workplace," Oleg stated. "I dined there once. It is an upscale establishment catering to downtown business types."

"You don't recall her?"

"No, but it was some time back. She may not have been on board."

Adam swung into the alley, easing his rental into a slot across from Alina's Ladel. They decided to kill a few minutes to give her prep time before she hit the dining floor.

"What do you suppose her position is here?" Adam asked. "Hostess? Manager? Waitress?"

"I'd rule out manager," Oleg said. "If she's not the hostess, she's a server. I suggest we ask to sit in Alina's section to confirm her first name no matter how certain you are it is her."

"Agreed."

They walked back down the alley to the restaurant's front entrance where a dapper man in a dark gray suit greeted them.

Oleg indicated which section they preferred, prompting the greeter to check his schedule before leading them to a dimly lit dining room and a corner booth. Moments later Alina was standing at their table handing them menus, looking no less stunning then when they first laid eyes on her an hour earlier. She had changed into uniform, an azure blue blouse and matching skirt rising pleasingly above the knee.

Yes, we're talking Julie Christie beauty, Adam concluded silently. Everything that is, except the warmth. Her ice blue eyes, peering from a pristine face light on makeup, reflected not only a pure beauty but a cool demeanor as well.

She turned to leave, returning a few minutes later.

"Excuse me. Do you speak English?" Adam asked her, bypassing his translator.

She lifted her eyes from the table she was setting. "Yes."

"Do you have a favorite item on the menu?" Adam asked.

"Many of our customers enjoy the pelmeni," she replied.

"And what is pelmeni?"

"They are like dumplings. They come in a thin pouch shaped like a honeycomb and are stuffed with combinations of fish or meat. You have your choice of either filling. They also come with sour cream and vinegar."

"They sound labor intensive," Adam said.

"It is the fast food of the Ukraine," Oleg interjected. "You chase them down with shots of vodka. They bring back nice memories of my youth. We ate them with our fingers. We also tried to suck the juice out of them before sinking our teeth into the cavity."

"Oh what fun you must have had." Adam directed his attention back to the server. "I'm more interested in what you like on the menu," he said.

"I prefer the Baikel omur. It comes fresh daily from the lake."

Alina's cool manner extended to her voice. Words flowed crisply from her tongue like cubes of ice from a vending machine.

Oleg handed her back the menu. They both followed her lead and settled on the omur.

"What do you think?" Adam asked, after she disappeared with the order.

"Of what?"

"Of her."

"Engaging she is not," Oleg said.

"Going through the motions? Like she would much rather be somewhere else?"

"Do you have a somewhere else in mind…somewhere with palm trees?"

"What if I should accidentally spill a drink on her to test her temperament?" Adam asked. "It may give us some insight into her."

"How would you like a drink spilled on you? It tests nothing. Russian people generally are very friendly, though many of them walk around with scowls on their faces."

"What do you know about this Lake Baikel? Adam asked.

"What do I know? It's the largest freshwater lake in the world. It's where this evening's dinner came from. It's so large it should be called a sea. In fact, it represents the making of an ocean as a result of the shifting of continents. It reaches depths of five thousand feet. It contains the largest volume of freshwater in the world. More than three hundred rivers and streams flow into it. The sole outlet is the Angara River, which by now you should be familiar with. It's so clear one can see forty meters down into the water. There are freshwater seals living in the lake. It freezes over in the wintertime with ice so thick the Trans-Siberian Railroad for a brief time was routed over it. Anything else you would like to know?" Oleg asked, halting his recitation.

"That's a little more than I was expecting," Adam said. "I take it the Baikel region must be on your guide itineraries."

Alina delivered the tea in her same expressionless manner while Oleg continued with his account. "I've taken many groups to the lake. It's a popular side trip for tourists traveling the Trans-Siberian. If we had more time, I would take you there. Regrettably, many tourists are unaware of as well as unprepared for the rawness of Baikel."

"In what way?" Adam asked.

"I once had a group of Portuguese tourists who insisted on taking a hike across the lake in January for the simple reason they could say they walked across Baikel. They didn't realize the problem was not falling through the ice. The problem was coming back without any toes due to frostbite, which was a guarantee. I did manage to talk them out of it after issuing the warning that they were doing it at their own risk."

"Does the lake thaw out for the summer tourist season?"

"Yes, and it's warm enough for hardy people to swim in it, which brings up one of the more interesting legends surrounding the lake, one our waitress brings to mind."

"Oh yeah?"

"The lake is so deep there are countless species of life found in its depths not found anywhere else in the world. Legend has it there are ice maidens, similar to mermaids, who swim the depths. On those occasions when wintertime arrives earlier than expected, an ice maiden every so often will become trapped in the thick ice cover, unable to escape to her lower realm. Some people---locals and tourists alike---swear to have seen their translucent figures frozen into the ice far below the surface. The legend goes on to say that when the thaw occurs and the ice maidens are freed, they are no longer able to survive the depths of Baikel and end up roaming the earth as humans. Now, I ask you. What are the chances our waitress and your potential suspect is an ice maiden?"

"You may be on to something," Adam said straight-faced. "Could be she's looking for a further thawing out in the States."

Oleg took a sip of tea. "And I'll give you one more bit of Baikel legend that should hit home with you," he said, clearly relishing his telling of tales. "On the southern tip of the lake sits a village called Kultuk. It's an hour's drive from here over a road that begins to deteriorate immediately outside Irkutsk. Five years ago I took a group of Americans on a tour of Baikel. The group included a marine biologist by the name of Robert Erin who was based somewhere in the Florida Keys. Erin has some Russian blood in him, which spurred his interest in seeing the marine life of Baikal. While here, he met an eccentric art gallery owner at the lake who had a cabin up for sale. Before returning home to the Keys, Erin told the owner he planned on buying the cabin, which he later did in a long distance transaction."

"What sort of cabin?" Adam asked.

"A nice one. A wooden cabin located not more than a hundred meters from the shore. It had a wood burning fireplace, tiny kitchen, a bedroom with a bunk, and bath. It was designed like an old, traditional Siberian hut. Erin was single and a sojourner at heart. He sold what few possessions he had back in the Keys, obtained a visa, returned to Baikel, and moved into the cabin on a permanent basis."

"He was prepared to give up his citizenship?" Adam asked.

"He really hadn't given it much thought in the beginning, feeling he had plenty of time to make that decision. Meanwhile, he had fallen in love with Baikel and felt it his destiny to move here."

"From Florida?" Adam asked, bewildered by the guy's decision.

"You'd be surprised where people will pick up from and head for," Oleg said. "It frequently happens as an offshoot of my tours. Of course, it doesn't always work out in the long run but it happens. They find happiness in the adventure of exploring new places and meeting different people."

"Come to think of it," Adam said, "it may not be all that preposterous. Shortly after I moved to Tampa, I took up with a young lady, a hair stylist, who was an avid stock car racing fan. On weekends we'd make the treks to Talladega, Daytona, or Homestead, or even some of the local dirt tracks. We'd sit in the infield among the throngs and while the cars circled the track, she'd point out to me the drivers, their positions, their strategies, and when they were due for a pit stop. Her devotion carried over to her apartment which was lined with racing paraphernalia---banners, magazine covers, photos, whatever."

"What may I ask were you doing spending time with her?" Oleg asked.

"That's what I asked myself the night she wore a checkered flag skirt and matching blouse on a dinner date. It was a quantum leap from the cut-off jeans and tank tops I normally saw her in. Not that the checkered flag outfit was the reason, but we mutually agreed to part ways once we recognized we did not have much in common. A year later I ran into her brother on the street and he informed me she had taken a vacation to London and fell in love with the place. She subsequently decided to move there to open a small antique shop with an English woman she had struck up a friendship with during her visit. I believe he said it was in the Mayfair section of town. My former girlfriend went from racecar groupie to London shopkeeper in the blink of an eye. There's an unlikely ex-patriot for you." Adam looked for a response from his dinner companion who was fast catching up on his eating. "Did you ever consider going the ex-patriot route, Oleg?"

"I don't consider myself a candidate, though someday I'd very much like to visit your country. Ukrainian roots run deep in our family's history. Unfortunately, the country resembles Poland in the hardships she has had to endure. Neighboring states and numerous ethnic groups are forever laying claims to portions of it. But not everyone in the region is determined to stay. It's recently become a trend for young women to migrate to the States on the promise of marriage from American men. From what I read and hear, many wind up trapped in rotten marriages, stranded in the streets, or dancing in men's clubs. It's a path I prefer my daughters not follow should they decide to set sail for the States."

From an adjacent dining area came a cacophony of voices engaged in a boisterous toast.

"The toast is the most popular part of the meal here," Oleg said.

"Sorry, I threw you off topic," Adam said. "Back to Erin. Did the move work out for him?"

"I kept in touch with him to see if he was adapting. I mean...here is this guy from Florida suddenly living in Siberia. As I said, I've seen many a long distance move but this one was at the far end of the spectrum."

"What was he living off of?"

"He had built up a little nest egg, plus he was able to take a couple of odd jobs to keep him afloat till he could find

122

something related to his marine biology credentials. The problem was he spoke very little Russian so his job prospects were limited. He did land a part-time job with one of the Baikel tour companies who catered to English-speaking nations. His marine biology background was a great help in that regard."

"When does the legend part kick in?" Adam asked, believing the move from the Keys to Siberia did not a legend make.

"It has to do with the golomyanka, another of the unique wonders of the lake," Oleg said. "It is a translucent fish, sparkling pink and blue in color. It is the most numerous fish in the lake and the favorite prey for other marine life, particularly the seals. It is a deepwater fish---real deep---and can only survive in temperatures up to plus five degrees centigrade. Because of their solitary lifestyle, they do not swim in mass formations. Therefore, they are difficult to catch in large quantities."

"So, what value do they have other than being a staple in the fish food chain?" Adam asked.

"Their value is that thirty-five percent of the fish contains medicinal oil, rich in vitamin A. Their fat can be melted down for use in the treatment of wounds. Heavy storms will wash many golomyanka ashore where the locals collect and haul them away. Well, once word got out regarding its healing powers, it wasn't long before Tibetan monks started drifting down from the top of the world to see what all the fuss was about. They could be seen strolling along the shores with all the other believers following storms. Among those who noticed their presence was Robert Erin. Now Erin was as much an adventurer and entrepreneur as he was a marine biologist. He was fully aware of the widespread interest in the region in the Tibetan methods of natural healing and saw the potential market for the medicinal oil. His business plan was simple. He would open up a fish market near Lake Baikel that would cater to the individual fisherman. They would bring their catch to him and he, in turn, would sell them to visitors, including the monks. He needn't worry about the big fish firms, since they could not build a volume business thanks to the solitary existence of the golomyanka."

"He had no problem obtaining business permits?"

"No. Russian officials saw no harm in it. In their view he was filling a little niche in the local economy, adding some revenue to it, and at the same time keeping the tourists intrigued with his see-through fish. Once he got the operation rolling, he became a local celebrity. A couple of Englishmen who were regular visitors to the lake took the y-a-n-k out of golomyanka and dubbed him Yankee Erin and the name stuck. Yankee Erin's Fish Market became a popular local hangout for fishermen, enabling Erin to carve out a living. However, it wasn't long before his wanderlust got the best of him, prompting him to use the business as a springboard to greater adventure. His golomyanka venture earned him favor with the monks and they ended up offering him an advisory position in their natural healing program, which they intended to export to other countries."

"He gave up the fish market?"

"Yes. He sold it and his cabin to a local fisherman and took off for Lhasa, the largest city in Tibet and the destination point for all the pilgrims in the country. The city sits above twelve thousand feet, so it can take the air out of a brain."

Adam grinned. "And it took it out of his?"

"We don't know. We never heard from him. Rumors began to fly he was coming back to Baikel to start up another business. There were also rumors of him becoming a Tibetan monk. One local claimed to have seen him donned in one of those familiar maroon robes, walking the shores of the lake with his fellow monks. None of the rumors proved true, however. Finally, a year or so ago I received a Christmas card from him. He was living in Manaus, Brazil, the main city along the Amazon River basin. He had taken up with a group of researchers who were conducting a study of another translucent fish...the candiru, one of the notorious fishes of the river."

"Notorious?" Adam said.

124

"Yes. If you're ever traveling the Amazon, make sure you never piss in it," Oleg said.

"The reason being?"

"The candiru swims upstream. I'll leave it at that," Oleg said. "I don't want to ruin your dinner."

Alina returned with their meals, still stingy with her smiles. Instead of chasing translucent fish, Yankee Erin might have been better served researching the translucent image of the ice maiden, Adam imagined. Alina Novikov was like frosted glass. One has no idea what's on the other side.

"I'm curious. Do many Americans dine here?" he asked her.

She hurled a quick glance to Oleg, as if to say 'why the hell are you not asking the questions.' "They stop in every so often," she answered dutifully.

"Mostly tourists, I suppose?" Adam asked, leaving Oleg out of the equation.

"A few businessmen," she said, ever so slightly leaning a hip against the table and crossing her arms. "Are you from America?"

"Yes. Florida to be specific."

Adam caught Oleg from the corner of his eye looking on in bemusement, undoubtedly wondering whether his client was prepared to push the button further in by mentioning the city he was from.

But raising suspicions was not Adam's intent. "Have you visited the States?" he asked.

"No," she said. "Maybe someday I will have the opportunity."

"And maybe someday I will come back here and try that pelmeni everyone is crazy about," Adam said.

Oleg leaned forward and whispered for both to hear. "Perhaps one day this young lady will invite you over for some home-cooked pelmeni."

"Sorry, I don't let strangers come into my home," she said, unlocking her arms and edging away from the table to resume her work.

"Nice try for whatever you were trying to elicit from her," Oleg said.

"A smile is all," Adam responded. A smile says a lot. I may have gotten one if you hadn't jumped in with that dumb suggestion."

"It was all in jest. Off hand, I'd say a smile was the furthest thing from her mind. You either need to work on your southern charm or accept the fact she has a heart as frozen as Lake Baikel."

Aloof though she was, they left her a generous tip. On their way back to her cottage they stopped at a merchandise store to purchase twenty-five feet of rope, a flashlight, and a flat iron.

•••

Adam again parked the car in the church parking lot, backing closer to the woods than previously. Tying the flat iron to the end of the rope, he noted the vehicle's odometer. "Did you realize we're further than fifteen kilometers from the railroad tracks?"

"Did you know people get stuck in chimneys?" Oleg responded.

"Are you saying this maneuver is a farcical one?" Adam asked.

His guide lowered his earflaps and tied them under his chin in preparation. "I couldn't have chosen a better word for it."

"Here's the way I look at it, Oleg. Eventually, we're going to be dead for a very, very long time. We might as well make the most of the living part while we can."

Adam coiled the rope around his shoulder. In the process, he imagined his former boss in the Florida Keys, enjoying his retirement, browsing the morning paper, his eyes falling on a brief story about a guy named Adam Fraley getting stuck in a chimney in faraway Siberia and dying. "It figures," he could hear his old boss mumble before flipping to the sports page.

126

They exited the car and circled through the woods toward Alina's cottage. Darkness had descended and with it came an increase in the intensity of the snowfall, heavy enough to shroud the landscape into a stillness, the sole sound that of the thick flakes lighting on the limbs of the closely spaced trees. They stopped at the outer edge of the woods, not more than fifteen yards from the cottage. In a low voice Adam instructed his guide. "Remember, if anyone shows up, you know nothing about this. As far as you're aware, I went into the woods to take a leak."

"And you remember...get in and get out," Oleg said, brushing specks of snow from his eyebrows.

A birch tree, sprouting branches like a three-pronged fork, abutted the cottage on the same side the chimney was located. It offered an easy climb to the roof. He shinnied up the tree and was at the chimney in no time. He hurriedly laid the coil of rope aside, took out the flashlight from his back pocket, and aimed it down the flue. Oleg was right. A mesh cap was fitted inside it. Gripping the fixture by hand, he yanked it three times before it came completely loose. He lifted it free and set it aside. He next took the rope and lowered the weighted end down the flue till it hit bottom nearly twenty feet below. As he hoisted it back up, he swung it back and forth in an attempt to detect any obstructions. With the entire rope back in hand, he detached the flatiron and tossed both in the direction of Oleg waiting at the edge of the woods. The guide grabbed the two items half-buried in the accumulating snow cover and headed back through the trees toward the car.

Adam mounted the chimney and lowered his legs into the top of the flue. Before he launched his downward movement, he retrieved the mesh cap he had set aside. Stretching his arms upward, he began his descent, discovering he had scarcely enough wiggle room to maneuver down. He pulled the mesh into place above him and lowered one hand to stretch his stocking cap completely over his head, something he would do when undergoing a closed MRI to help ward off an attack of

127

claustrophobia. Again he extended both arms straight up, simultaneously pressing his palms flat against the sides of the flue and pushing downward while at the same time wiggling his frame in the same direction. Two hand lengths let him know he had traveled a foot. Fifty hand lengths and he should hit bottom.

He was making good progress, but misfortune struck when he reached the thirty-hand-mark and he had nobody to blame but himself. Rather than keeping the flashlight in hand, he had shoved it into his back pocket and forgot about it. As he wiggled down the flue, the flashlight wiggled up and joined with his jeans to create a wedge. In effect, it served as a door jam, halting further movement. He wiggled his butt again, again, and again to no avail. He tried to move an arm behind his back, but after much straining, the best he could do was reach a forefinger and a middle finger to the tip of his pocket. Freeing the flashlight was not unlike removing a fat wallet from a thin pocket, except in this instance he had no free hand to execute the feat.

He had passed the point of no return. There was no going back up. Should he have asked Oleg to remain at the chimney top with the rope? It would have made no difference, he reasoned. A brawny bodybuilder would not be able to haul him up from the position he was in, much less his spindly guide. Moreover, the decision had been made to keep Oleg's involvement to a minimum.

Adam slipped his stocking cap above his eyes. It may have worked during an MRI exam but there he could fold his arms and imagine clearance. Here his hands reminded him that the scant clearance he had was gone. He knew the anxiety attack was about to wash over him like a tsunami at any moment, rendering him helpless to the gripping fear that would follow. He pressed his hands against the flue and rested his forehead against them. He slowly inhaled and exhaled in an effort to breathe the anxiety out of him. More than anything else, the simple exercise reminded him he was still alive, able to concentrate, and that another breathing human waiting outside in a car had his back.

Adam concentrated on his back. He reached down to unfasten his belt, unbutton his pants button, and unzip his zipper to loosen his jeans. Tugging and wiggling, he attempted to ride the flashlight to the small of his back above his butt. Half inch by half inch he managed to maneuver the lump to the pit of his back. He next refastened his fly and jeans and again pushed downward, this time producing some movement. The clearance he created was miniscule yet sufficient to lessen his anxiety and lift his spirits. He resumed his downward crawl, but instead of foot by foot, it was inch by inch. At last, he felt his feet clear the flue, followed by his legs and the remainder of his torso, his ass landing on the grate, his flailing legs knocking over the protective screen. Scrambling out from under the pit, he quickly put everything back in order. Free of the fireplace, he paused to take several deep breaths, overjoyed at his triumph. His joy was short-lived, however, when a shout from outside the cottage split the silence.

"What the hell," he whispered.

A second shout and a third followed...in Russian. It sounded like somebody's name being called. "Alina! Alina!" Was that it?

He took the flashlight from his back pocket and rushed through the house, aiming its beam in every direction. He avoided the temptation to pry into rooms, though he could not help but note the overall tidy condition of the place. "A Spartan atmosphere...clean and orderly with a bold feminine flavor," he whispered below the clamor.

The shouts continued. "Alina...Alina!"

Along with the cries, came the blasts of a car horn. It was Oleg no doubt, trying to make him aware of the situation outside. It reminded him of the episode on Murin's street and the folly of both.

Adam searched for a desk or table, something she might place correspondence on.

"Alina...Alina!" The shouts this time were accompanied by a pounding on the door.

Adam skipped from the kitchen to the bedroom where, on top of a dresser, he found what he was after, an envelope with Murin's return address on the front. Snatching the prize, he bolted for the back of the house. In his haste he tripped over a suitcase resting against a closet wall and landed on all fours. Regaining his footing he resumed his dash to the rear door, sliding back the dead bolt, and stepping outside into near blizzard conditions. Carefully closing the door behind him, he jogged around the corner of the house where he caught sight of Oleg waiting with the rental car in the middle of the street. Thick snowflakes angled through the vehicle's bright beams. Loping toward it in the deepening ground cover, he ran smack into the night caller, a hefty figure of a man who looked at him in stunned surprise before snarling something and hurling a near empty bottle of vodka his way, missing wildly.

"Come on...get in!" Oleg yelled from the opened window of the car.

Adam scrambled into the Ladel and the two took off, as another vodka bottle sailed past the driver's side window.

"For God's sake! Where's he coming up with all the booze," Adam snapped.

"It's the lifeblood of this country and as readily available as water," Oleg said, as he stamped on the accelerator.

For some distance the low-charging hulk gave chase, barking at them like a neighborhood mutt at the heels of a passing car.

"Where did Boris come from?" Adam asked, brushing fresh snow from his clothes.

"From the house next door."

"No wonder she wants to get the hell out of here."

Adam checked the side view mirror to see Boris standing in the middle of the street, having given up the chase, his fists pounding the air.

"Any luck inside?" Oleg asked.

130

"Maybe. I didn't have much time with all the commotion going on." Adam reached into his pocket and pulled out the letter. "I did find this, though."

"Have you read it?" Oleg asked.

"First of all, I didn't have time to read anything. I was following your advice to get in and get out. Secondly, I think it's safe to say it's in Russian. Want to pull over and take a look?"

"Let's first drop this car off at the rental place. We can read it at our leisure afterward."

Not until they were back in the rail station waiting room did Adam anxiously fish the letter from his pocket and hand it to Oleg.

"Don't get your hopes up," his guide forewarned, taking the envelope and peeling out its contents, which turned out to be a single page of stationery. "Ready?" he asked.

"Read the damn thing."

Oleg glanced at the letter prior to reading it. "It's more of a message than a letter," he said.

"What's the message then?"

My dearest Alina,

The path to our happiness is now open. She was easy to take care of. There is little else to say at this time, other than I look forward to seeing you soon.

Love always,

Alexei

"Is it dated?" Adam asked.

"March 6," Oleg replied.

Adam extended his hand. "Let me take a look." Oleg handed it over, whereupon he scanned the page. "Are you sure of the translation?"

"Positive. Should bring smiles all around back home...right?"

Adam slipped the letter and envelope back into his pocket. "Yes, except for one certain detective."

CHAPTER TEN

The skies cleared overnight, leaving the morning sun to cast a harsh, dazzling glare across the railroad station platform where Adam and Oleg stood under a vendor's Coca Cola umbrella enjoying a steaming hot breakfast of tea, sausage, and boiled potatoes.

"I'd have booked an earlier train but this was the only available one," Oleg said.

"Still sticking to your get in and get out theme, are you?"

"As I mentioned before, there is a palpable nervousness in this country, what with all the geopolitical stuff going on in the world," Oleg said. "There's no telling how it will manifest itself on the local level. I think it best to expect the unexpected."

In many ways Oleg reminded Adam of his old boss. He had a nose for the street and the people who populated it, never underestimating their ability to outsmart you, while at the same time mindful of their intention to do so. In this regard both Oleg and his former boss were of one mind.

They finished breakfast, gathered their luggage, and headed for the waiting room to await their train due in forty-five minutes. They picked out a bench and in five minutes Adam was half asleep when he felt an elbow in the ribs.

"Don't look now but is that who I think it is sitting at the far end of the bench across from us?" Oleg asked.

Adam looked down the row of waiting passengers.

"The big, bald guy with the meaty face," Oleg added.

He finally spotted the man who immediately glared back at him. "Wouldn't you know it, of all the days and trains Boris has to choose from, he picks this one."

"Not so unusual," Oleg said. "The weekends are a popular travel time. Like I said, for the locals the Trans-Siberian is often the only reasonable travel option between towns."

Adam attempted to avoid the guy's glare but felt it nonetheless.

"He's trying to figure out where he knows us from," Oleg said.

"Whether he recognizes us or not, it's clear he doesn't like our looks," Adam said.

"Do you have any personal items in your baggage you can't afford to lose?" Oleg asked.

"No...you're thinking he's going to run off with our baggage?" Adam asked.

"I'm considering all the possibilities. He's spoiling for a fight."

Not unexpectedly, Boris barked something out to them.

"'Are you happy with the breakup of our mother country,' he's asking you," Oleg said.

Adam ignored the question.

In a sudden display of bravado, Boris stood up and addressed the other passengers awaiting the train, jabbing his finger in Adam's and Oleg's direction. "He's calling us subversives, instigators, CIA agents, out to destroy Mother Russia," Oleg dutifully reported.

"We're traveling platskartny class, or whatever you call it, back to Moscow, are we not?" Adam asked. "We won't exactly be The Traveling Wilburys with him aboard."

"Who are The Traveling Wilburys?" Oleg asked.

"I'll fill you in later."

Plainly smarting from the inattention he was getting, Boris kept up his bullying, building up tension among waiting passengers who were trying their best to ignore his outbursts.

As if in reaction to his frustration, Adam absentmindedly took out his stocking cap and yanked it on, realizing too late it was just the thing to trigger Boris's memory.

"Alina! Alina!" he shouted, jumping to his feet. A moment later he was lumbering toward Adam, his mouth frothing and fists clinched, as bystanders looked on in trepidation.

Adam rose to meet him but Oleg beat him to the punch, springing into the path of the oncoming hulk and jabbing him in the chest with a forefinger. Words flew between the two, each exchange escalating the vitriol and chest jabs, which were turning into shoves.

Adam stepped in, reaching for Oleg's shoulder. "Oleg...Oleg...take it easy. Let me handle it," he said.

But Oleg would have none of it. He continued to lash out, his normally placid face flushed red with anger, his breath vented word by word till he had no breath left.

All at once, Oleg backed away from the ogre towering over him, placing his hand over his chest and gasping for air.

"Oleg...Oleg! What's wrong?" Adam asked, watching his travel mate slump to the floor.

Startled into inaction by the development, Boris took a step back and gave the two of them a good riddance flick of the wrist before returning to his seat.

"Somebody call an ambulance!" Adam yelled out. No one seemed to understand or wanted to be involved so he ran to the nearest service desk to repeat his demand. "Call an ambulance! Call security! Someone's ill!"

Adam rushed back to Oleg and crouched at his side. "Hang on buddy," he said.

Station security arrived first followed soon after by an emergency vehicle crew. The responders hurriedly examined Oleg but gave no indication of his condition. Adam insisted on accompanying him in the ambulance. Sitting in the back of the unit, images of the man's family back in the Ukraine awaiting his return occupied his mind. Perhaps it was his Ukrainian patriotism that led him to confront the Russian boor, Adam speculated. Whatever, by now their train to Moscow had left the station, stranding the two in Irkutsk.

Adam gazed out the rear window of the ambulance to the trailing street traffic scene. They had arrived in Irkutsk less than two days ago but already the city was beginning to feel like a home away from home. He returned his attention to Oleg whose eyes presently were open and whose face bore a half smile...an unmistakably wry one.

Adam glared at his guide. "You son-of-a-bitch," he said.

Oleg's half smile widened to a full one.

"You son-of-a-bitch," Adam repeated, dragging it out.

"You didn't think I was going to board that train with Boris on it, did you?" he said.

They ended up with a short stay in the hospital, Oleg insisting he was fine, the doctors agreeing.

"What now?" Adam asked.

"We're going to take a taxi to the city center and catch a bus to Litvyanka. We're adding another leg to our journey."

"What's to see in Litvyanka?"

"When I was talking to Darya Pronin yesterday, she mentioned in passing a boyhood friend of Alex Murin who presently resides there. He may be able to provide more background information for you."

"Where's it located?"

"On the northern rim of Lake Baikel. It's the nearest point from here to the lake," Oleg said. "And there's a second reason to make the visit. It would be a shame for you to travel all this way and not see the lake."

"How long a trip is it?" Adam asked.

"A little over an hour. It's an easy day trip. The buses run regularly between here and there. We should be back to Irkutsk by evening."

"What are the chances of Boris showing up on the bus?" Adam asked, not entirely in jest.

"Boris will not be on the bus nor will he be waiting for one," Oleg said, suppressing a smile. "At least I don't think so."

●●●

With its drab and cramped interior, the Irkutsk bus station was in keeping with general bus-station décor. Adding to its unkempt appearance was a major electrical repair job underway. A large portion of the terminal's false ceiling had been removed, exposing loose cables, a number of which dangled not far above waiting passengers' heads. Fortunately, the wait was brief for Adam and Oleg, as the off-season ticket lines were nearly non-existent. By late morning, they were traveling the road to Baikel aboard a workhorse of a bus half-filled with passengers. "Day laborers making the commute to earn a few bucks at jobs that go begging," Oleg observed.

A sightseeing excursion it was not, as sealed, grime covered windows combined with the haze of a late winter's day to draw a curtain on the outside world. Soon, the warmth of the carriage and whirr of tires induced a sleep in Adam, at times interrupted by the jars from potholes, stretches of knobby road, or the snores of a trio of slumbering coach mates.

A grip on his shoulder awoke Adam. "We're here," Oleg said.

Stepping off the bus, Adam noted the haze had dissipated, raising the curtain on a scene Oleg described as unique to the natural world. Stretching to the horizon in every direction as far as the eye could see was a sea of solid ice glistening pearl blue under the midday sun. A force of nature, if there ever was one, Adam thought, taking in the sight.

"I'm going to duck inside the station and give that boyhood pal of Murin's a call," Oleg said, taking leave.

The smell of smoked fish wafting from across the way drew Adam's attention to a flea market located on the main square. A scattering of customers surveyed the offerings in much the same manner as the Trans-Siberian riders contemplated the displays of the railroad platform vendors.

For Adam, the provincial scene took on an ominous cast when two men wearing visors, dark green jackets with shoulder boards, colored insignias, and sleeve patches emerged from behind a small cluster of customers and crossed the road in his direction. Perhaps they took him for a loiterer or a petty thief in waiting, standing there all alone, casing out the place, or maybe it was for something more sinister, something along the lines of what Boris accused him of back at the rail station. He was convinced it had nothing to do with the home invasion, as recent as it was. Whatever the reason, the two were making a beeline for him.

The older and stouter of the two addressed him first in a tone as crisp as the air they were breathing. Adam's response was to dig out his visa and hand it to the guy, who carefully scanned it before turning it over to his younger and leaner partner. In turn, the younger one said something to which Adam pleaded ignorance by throwing open his hands.

"Let me handle this," came words in English from behind him, as Oleg arrived with a box of chocolates in hand.

Adam turned onlooker as the three talked it over. At one point, Oleg pulled out his identification to display it to his inquisitors, triggering another round of inspections. Finally, they handed it back to his guide and sauntered off, but not before casting one last glance at the two travelers.

"What was that all about?" Adam asked.

"It's all about nothing," Oleg said. "They are members of the militsiya or Soviet militia. They are known to harass people for no good reason. They are universally disliked by the locals and are probably not long for the world once the Soviet Union completes its breakup."

"Thanks for the chocolates," Adam said, extending his hand.

A smile slowly formed on his guide's face. Standing there with his earflaps down, he looked like an emaciated hound sporting outsized ears. "They're for Kristina Kozlov, wife of Valentin Kozlov," he said, hugging the box against his side.

"Murin's boyhood pal?"

"Yes. I was able to get hold of him while you were experiencing the charms of the militsiya. He invited us over to his cabin, which is not far from here, a mile and a half at most," he said. "Follow me."

Listvyanka's main road was one long street, which also served as an embankment. They walked north along the avenue until it narrowed into a pathway jutting into the hills.

"Keep an eye out for verglas," Oleg said.

"What the hell is verglas?" Adam asked.

"Sorry…black ice to you. It forms on the rocks."

Navigating one icy patch of trail after another, they reached the crest of the first hill where they paused to absorb the full spectacle stretched out before them. In addition to the vast expanse of ice that was the lake, countless cabins could be seen lining the shore, the smoke from their chimneys crooking skyward in light shades of gray.

"It's an entirely different scene in the summertime," Oleg observed from his side.

"I prefer it this way," Adam said, his face flushed by the sweep of the wind across the hillsides. "There's something to be said for the raw beauty of it."

Reaching the top of the second hill, Oleg pulled a map from his pocket to check their position. "That must be their cabin down there," he said, pointing to the foot of the rise they stood upon.

Adam vigorously patted his reddened cheeks. "Home and hearth await. Let's go."

•••

In outward appearance Valentin and Kristina Kozlov were a match. Both cut handsome figures in their brown suede jackets and pants. They also sported similar hairstyles…light brown hair trimmed super short so as not to hide clear complexions, so it appeared to Adam. It certainly wasn't the grizzle and garb he was expecting.

"Please…please, have a seat," Valentin said in easy English.

It was a comfortable one-bath cabin with a full kitchen, a twin set of bunk beds, and a hot tub. Adam commandeered one of the two armchairs adjacent to the stone fireplace.

Valentin took the other, leaving a small couch for Oleg and Kristina. Centered on the floor between them was an open-mouthed bearskin rug close to six feet in length from nose to tail. Curled up asleep on the hide was an ash-coated Siberian husky ostensibly undisturbed by the activity around him.

"Is this your first visit to Lake Baikel, Adam?" Valentin asked.

"Yes, and it's beautiful," he said

No sooner had Adam settled in than he came under the spell of the fireplace, its warmth and flickering light slipping him into a semi-conscious state where the present and the past drifted in and out in shapeless form. He leaned back and stretched his shoeless feet toward the hearth, wiggling the cold out of his toes.

"What's the dog's name?" Oleg asked.

"Sheriff," Valentin said, pronouncing the "i" like an "ee."

"As in Omar Sharif?" Adam asked, his mind back on Julie Christie.

"No, Sheriff as in the Sheriff of Dodge City," Oleg deadpanned.

"I'm a big fan of American westerns," Valentin explained.

Adam felt like curling up with Sheriff on the bear rug.

"Are fireplaces common in Florida?' Valentin asked.

"About as common as air conditioners are here, I would imagine," Adam answered.

A smile crossed Oleg's face. "Adam's still trying to figure out how Santa is able to squeeze down a chimney," he said.

"Ha!" Valentin whooped. "Our Father Frost is much too smart to climb down chimneys and land on hot coals. He prefers to show up at holiday parties and hand out the gifts."

Kristina Kozlov served hot tea and chocolates while her husband jumped from topic to topic, each contributing to Adam's torpid state. With Valentin doing all the talking, it left the impression his wife spoke no English or else she would have snuck in a word or two by this time. Whether she understood it was another question.

"Oleg tells me you are an acquaintance of Alexei Murin," Valentin said, yanking Adam out of his stupor.

"Yes, and I understand he was a boyhood friend of yours," he responded.

"He was, for sure," Valentin said. "We grew up together in Irkutsk. But then his family picked up and moved to Omsk."

"That was the last you saw of him?" Oleg asked.

"Oh, no. We kept in touch. Later on I decided to enroll in the police academy he was attending in Omsk. We were not in the same class but we hung out together. It was there I met Kristina," he said, nodding to his wife sitting demurely in the glow of the flickering light with teacup in hand.

"Alexei was not so fortunate in finding a wife?" Oleg asked.

"Ha!" Valentin whooped again. "What's the old saying? He was like a kid in a candy store. He had his choice of women. Believe it or not, it turned out to be a problem for him, one most men would like to have. Women were too easy for him, even the smart ones, and it was a smart one he wanted."

"Why didn't he settle for one? Adam asked

Valentin took a sip of tea and leaned back in his armchair. "He never found an intelligent one he liked. Plus, there was always the beautiful Alina in the back of his mind."

"Alina?" Adam asked, feigning ignorance.

"Yes, his childhood sweetheart and the girl he swore he would someday marry."

"Why didn't he?" Oleg asked, nudging the line of conversation along.

Valentin threw up his arms. "Who knows? I lost touch with him when Kristina and I married and returned to this area. It was always our wish to make Baikel our home."

"And Alexei Murin moved to America," Oleg said. "Do you know his reason for doing so?"

"Yes," Valentin declared. "Yankee Erin."

Adam and his guide exchanged glances.

"You do know Yankee Erin, don't you?" Valentin asked, directing the question to Oleg.

"Yes, I do."

"Some years ago Alexei was visiting Irkutsk and stopped over to say hello. During his visit I introduced him to Yankee Erin who enchanted him with stories of Florida. According to a mutual acquaintance, it wasn't long after that he decided to start a new life in America."

"He left Alina behind?" Adam pointedly asked.

Valentin shook his head. "I'm sure he planned on bringing her over later. He probably needed to establish himself first."

From what Valentin was saying, he was unaware Murin married an American girl. Neither Adam nor Oleg mentioned the fact.

"Is he enjoying Florida?" Valentin asked.

"It appears so," Adam replied.

"Ol' Alexei...he was a good guy. We had lots of fun together."

A pop from the fireplace drew everyone's attention to the pulsating embers.

"Time to fetch some more logs," Valentin said, vacating his chair to head for the door.

A silence settled over the room. Adam noted how Kristina's eyes darted back and forth between the three men during the course of the conversation. She may not have participated, but not all of the meaning escaped her, Adam was convinced.

"Oleg, ask her if she also thinks Alex Murin was a good guy," Adam said, breaking the silence.

Oleg hiked his eyebrows in a show of surprise before turning to Kristina to repeat the question. In response, her eyes quickly moved from Oleg, to Adam, to the doorway. "Nyet," she said with firmness, while wearing a pained look on her face. "Nyet."

The door reopened and Valentin entered clutching an armful of logs before an explanation from Kristina could be cajoled. He tossed several of the logs onto the embers. The others he placed on a log holder. Finished with his chore, he turned to face his guests. "Time for banya!" he said and slapped his hands in glee.

Adam looked to Oleg for meaning. "A Russian sauna," his guide said.

Before they had a chance to decide whether it was a good idea or not, Valentin was tossing them two large white towels.

Kristina discreetly moved to the kitchen and turned her back to them, as the three shed their clothes. Towels in place, they followed Valentin outside to a flat stone path leading to a tiny wooden building abutting the rear of the cabin.

"What's the routine?" Adam asked Oleg in a low voice while attempting to appear nonchalant in stepping over the ice-covered stones. "You sweat it out for fifteen or twenty minutes and then you rush outside to take a leap into a snow bank," he answered. "If you survive the first round, you repeat it a second time."

Valentin escorted them into the single-room structure. "I've already got it warmed up," he said, shutting the door behind them.

Lined along the floor of the building were four body-length benches. In one corner of the room stood a stove. Between its firebox and water tank, there was a chamber to house the rocks. Alongside the stove sat a large wooden bucket filled to the brim with water. Valentin took a smaller bucket sitting next to it, filled it with water from the larger one and with a single heave emptied it onto the rocks, generating a loud hiss and cloud of steam reaching to the ceiling.

"Take to the benches," Valentin instructed his guests, "and drop the towels."

They followed their host's instructions, discarding the towels and prostrating themselves on the warm slabs of wood. From the corner of his eye, Adam watched Valentin continue to pitch water over the rocks, spraying steam in every direction until it thickened the room. The Russian next took a handful of leaved twigs from a pile on the floor, dipped them into the bucket of cold water, and proceeded to smack his guests over their bodies from neck to foot. "Helps clean the skin," he said between lashes.

In short time the two guests were sweating profusely. Adam guessed the temperature in excess of a hundred.

"Attention! Attention!" Valentin called out through the mist. "Time for your outdoor break." The Russian swung open the door. Oleg immediately jumped to his feet and darted for the entrance with Adam close on his heels. The two raced toward the nearest snow bank and plunged their naked bodies into the deep mound of packed flakes. While Oleg executed some weird kind of butterfly stroke over and over, Adam performed a breaststroke of sorts, astonished how he went from a sweating state to a shivering one with no step in-between.

"Indoors! Indoors!" Valentin shouted, holding the door open for them. Another sprint and they were back face down on the benches, sweating or melting Adam wasn't sure.

"What exactly does this do for you?" Adam breathlessly whispered to his guide, as Valentin watered the rock once more.

"Supposedly, it increases the red blood cells, hemoglobin, and oxygen levels," Oleg answered. "It's also a way of purging the impurities from the body. It's the way people clean themselves in this part of the world."

And since they survived the first round, there was a second round.

"Now for the piece de resistance," Valentin said at the end of the second round. The Russian stood by the stove with an opened bottle of vodka, which he raised high before he emptied it onto the rocks, shooting another cloud of steam into the air along with an odor foreign to Adam's olfactory sense. "Banya is finished," Valentin said with a flourish, after which the trio gingerly tiptoed back to the cabin.

"We should go ice fishing this afternoon," the Russian said upon their return. "I hear the bullheads are biting."

"Thank you for the offer," Oleg said, "but we must be heading back to the station, if we are to catch the last bus to Irkutsk."

"Then how about lunch before you leave? Kristina can heat up a pot of borsch and fix us smoked fish sandwiches."

"Sounds appetizing," Oleg said, "but we really must be headed out. We are on a tight time schedule."

"If it were summertime, I would give you a boat ride to the station," Valentin said. "It would save you much time."

Adam took Oleg's lead and stood to leave, reaching out to shake the couples' hands. "Spasiba...spasiba," he said vigorously, and followed Oleg out the door.

•••

"We'll take a taxi from the Irkutsk bus station to the airport and hop a plane to Moscow," his guide said, as they hiked the trail back. "Fortunately, the airport is within the city limits and a short jaunt from the Irkutsk central station. I know you are on a tight budget but the plane ride will be on me. It was my choice."

"At least we'll be traveling light, though things could get a bit gamy for those sitting around us," Adam said, as he gingerly navigated the icy patches of trail.

Back in Moscow they parted ways. Fast friends they had become, it went without saying. Adam's former boss long ago advised him there would be no shortage of disreputable characters he would encounter in his chosen line of work, but every so often, he would run into a good one along the way. Oleg Popov was one of the good ones.

CHAPTER ELEVEN

Tamra fully expected Alex Murin to give her a call. Whether she wanted him to or not depended on the time of day and which side of the debate raging in her mind she was on---the side telling her to let his actions be her guide or the side telling her to sit this one out. To ease the debate, she concentrated on her duties, which consisted of running a spreadsheet, compiling schedules, organizing computer files, and ordering office supplies. She also fielded a couple of requests from attorneys for de-bugging and anti-wiretapping jobs, chores she was not sure they handled. She put them in her question mark file along with a note reminding her to clarify with Adam exactly what job requests were acceptable according to the guidelines provided her. "Don't drop us in the middle of a mess" was hardly a helpful instruction.

Over her lunch hour, she decided to do a little detection work herself, hustling over to the downtown public library to conduct some research in past issues of the Bay Area Beacon newspaper. Scanning an index to the paper, she found an entry for September 22, 1988. Jotting down the citation, she handed it to a librarian. A few minutes later, the copy was in her hand. She flipped to the cited page number and found the headline she was in search of.

Detective Receives Commendation

...Law enforcement officials yesterday presented Detective Alex Murin of the sheriff's department with a letter of commendation for meritorious service relating to an incident on August 17, 1988. Responding to an emergency call, Detective Murin was able to apprehend without the use of

147

force a suicidal person threatening to take his own life and those of his wife and two children with a homemade explosive device. In April of this year, Detective Murin was awarded a commendation letter for utilizing his investigative and communication skills to bring about the release of two hostages and the peaceful surrender of an escaped convict.

Tamra made a copy of the article, returned the paper to the librarian, and left for her office. On arriving she checked for messages. There were none.

By late afternoon her great expectations had given way to sober resignation. All for the better, perhaps. She now could spend the weekend relaxing with a book instead of dealing with fanciful talk. For her, reading had become the ideal antidote to social angst. She may not have the degrees, but she could thank any number of ex suitors for the education in life she had received.

At a quarter to five, she scrambled to straighten up the office before the five o'clock closing time. At four fifty-nine the call came.

"Hello Tamra," he said in a relaxed tone.

"Hello Alex."

"So here's my wish for the weekend," he said right off. "I'm day-tripping tomorrow morning to a special place few people in these parts know exists. It would make the trip a lot more special if you were to accompany me."

"Special in what way?" she asked and quickly added, "I mean the place, not me."

"My describing it does not do it justice," he said. "It has to be experienced."

She knew the difference between cockiness and confidence in a man, the difference that can determine for a woman a yes or a no to a request for a date. Furthermore, she was always a sucker for adventure, especially when it was spiced with surprise.

"And what would I wear to this special place?" she asked.

"Casual-outdoors. Where do I come get you?"

"Here at the office is fine."

"I'll see you at eight in the morning."

•••

He defined the image of casualness, one arm dangling out the opened window of his late model jeep, the other resting on the back of the passenger seat. It was the image Alex Murin greeted her with as she pulled into the parking lot aside him.

"Hop in," he said, extending an arm to open the passenger door.

He was dressed in a white t-shirt and faded jeans, a combo Tamra came close to matching with her off-white pullover and denims.

In no time they were headed east on the interstate. A half hour later they exited south onto a lightly traveled shell rock road leading to a third pathway which was little more than weed infested twin ruts carved out over time by wheels. For the next half hour they navigated the narrow tracks, past stands of hardwood and pine, cabbage palms, drooping willows, and a dun-colored stream meandering through thick underbrush.

By and by they traversed a long, sweeping curve in the road, skirting a breadth of dense woods at which point her escort eased the jeep onto a level patch of land approximate to the road.

"Here we are. " He said.

She looked about, noting nothing special. "Is this the place?"

"Not quite. We have a short walk yet to take."

She trailed him down the semblance of a footpath, through clusters of cypress trees draped with Spanish moss, so thickset it had to be parted like curtains. A final parting opened to their view a vision of a Florida pocket Eden.

"Oh my, Alex," she said.

"Locals call it 'The Veiled Lagoon,'" he said.

"The Veiled Lagoon," she slowly repeated, absorbing the vision.

A phalanx of moss-laden cypress and live oak trees closely encircled the lagoon, their shadowed reflections clearly visible on the water's placid surface. Along the shallow edges, reeds and rushes intermingled with yellow and white water lilies.

He took her hand and led her to a grassy mound rising above the banks.

"My easy chair," he said, patting the ground in an invitation to join him.

"How did you discover this place?" she asked.

"Stumbled across it while investigating a case a couple of years ago. This was once part of Tampa Bay but over time it became separated by winds, waves, and tides."

"The bay is not far from here?" she asked.

"Not far. We made the long semi-circle to the eastern side of it. The sole access road is the one we took." He pointed a finger to the west. "There are mangrove islands galore and some leftover sand dunes between the lagoon and the bay. I understand at one time this was all farmland. A large portion of it has since been set aside as protected land."

"The water looks so clean," she said.

"You can thank the storm-water management people for that," he said. "Along with taking measures to prevent runoff pollution from entering, they dug two culverts from the bay to the lagoon to allow the tides to periodically flush it with clean water."

"You said you were investigating a case. What kind of case?"

"Missing person. Nothing came of it."

"Do you come here often?"

"Now and then. I consider it a sanctuary…a personal refuge from the outside world."

A light wind brushed through the Spanish moss, sending ripples across the lagoon's surface.

"See the sunlight filtering through the strands of moss?" he asked. "At sunrise and sunset the veils begin to resemble strings of Chinese lanterns casting an ethereal glow over the interior. It gives the water a phosphorescent look."

"Like stained glass windows to the interior of a church," she observed.

"Can you smell a woodsy fragrance?" he asked

"Yes, I can," she responded enthusiastically. "What is it?"

"There are tiny yellow-green flowers attached to the base of the Spanish moss leaves. They give off a light aroma…an earthy scent. You can especially detect it at night."

"You come here at night?" she asked.

"On occasion…at night you can hear the nightingales compete in song with the mockingbirds, and, by the way, you can also see ghosts."

Tamra widened her eyes. "Woo…ghosts," she said. "What was the last ghost you saw?"

"I saw the ghost cat," he said matter-of-factly.

"A kitty cat? How frightening can that be? In all seriousness, Alex, what exactly is a ghost cat?"

"A Florida Panther. It's nearly extinct, though there are still occasional sightings of them."

"Including one by you here at The Veiled Lagoon?" she asked.

"See those tall cattails lined up over there along the edge of the opposite shore?" he asked, pointing across the lagoon.

"Yes."

"One night I was sitting right here, taking in the sounds and scents, when I spotted through the cattails this pair of burning white eyes slowly moving laterally along the shore. His eyes appeared fixed on me, until he stooped to drink. Then the burning eyes would disappear and reappear a moment later when he finished.

"How do you know it was a panther?"

"The cat was of fairly good size…bigger than a bobcat for sure. Their primary domain is south of here but they do range up to two hundred miles or so."

"So, there are some left?"

"Very few, apparently. I was reading where wildlife officials are planning to bring in some cougars from elsewhere to stabilize the gene pool."

"Did he see you?"

151

"He may not have seen me, but he no doubt scented me. He was downwind."

"You had no fear of him? He wasn't hissing or snarling?"

"No fear whatsoever. While the cat was here, there was an absolute silence that fell over the lagoon…no animal sounds to be heard…nothing to draw my attention from his eyes moving in the darkness."

"You were too concentrated on his eyes to hear anything, Alex."

He turned to her. "I do have a tendency to fixate on eyes," he said.

"The cat just wandered off after getting his drink?" she asked, brushing a wisp of hair away.

"Yes. Took his drink and quietly left."

"I hope he stays safe in his travels."

"He will until he crosses a highway. He then becomes unfair game for the motorists."

He took her hand and gently stroked it.

"Alex, what is the name of the woman back in Russia?" she dared ask.

"Alina."

"Tell me about her."

He paused, as if to collect his thoughts. "Picture this place frozen over," he said, releasing his hands from hers and framing them in front of him. "Substitute snow-covered spruce trees for the cypress and live oak, ice formations for the Spanish moss, and a thick-ribbed ice cover for the water. Both are beautiful but only one evokes a passion."

Tamra turned her gaze from a motionless ibis standing in the reeds preparing to strike to her companion. He in turn found her lips with his amid a veil of windblown hair. Impulsively, she engaged his kiss, allowing an ember of passion to course its way through her.

They sat a while in silence, listening to the calls of a myriad of water birds.

"Alex, I don't want to be a part of a betrayal," she said, ending the interim.

"Betrayals follow vows. They don't precede them."

"Engagements?"

"What is an engagement other than a probation?"

"Can I ask about your wife?"

He again took her hand in his. "Former wife...sure. Her name was Vickie."

"How did you and Vickie end up together?"

"I was the stranger in the strange land and when you're a stranger, you try your best not to be one. You attempt to find a niche in society to fit into and in the process you learn the best way to facilitate the fitting is to find a friend. Vickie became that friend. She then became my wife."

"Your first face-to-face meeting with her took place where?" she asked.

"Believe it or not, it was our mutual interest in the theater that brought us together. I was a frequent patron of the Starlight Dinner Theater where Vickie regularly performed. One day I ran into her by chance at the grocery store and struck up a conversation, which resulted in a date and eventually in a marriage."

"Were you and Vickie much alike?"

"We were in some ways. Interestingly enough, we approached our stage roles in a different manner---"

"Your stage roles?" she interjected.

"Yes, long ago I played stage roles while in school back home. Nothing came of it, but I enjoyed the experience of surrendering my identity for that of another. And therein was the difference in the way we approached the stage. Vickie could lose herself in a role but not to the point of surrendering her identity. She was back to being Vickie the instant the final curtain was lowered, prepared to adopt the next identity offered her. On the other hand, a character could capture my identity, which is the reason I had difficulty transitioning to other roles. My last play was an adaptation of The Brothers Karamazov. I played Dimitri, except it would be more accurate to say I was and am to this day Dimitri Karamazov...passionate and at times intemperate...not always good traits when you're chasing down the bad guys."

He paused and let out a deep breath. "So, to answer your question. Vickie, while a good person, was unlike me in seeking passion in life. She was lukewarm, which is not in the Russian character."

He took both of her hands and wrapped them in his. "But you, Tamra, are much like me. I am certain of this. Whatever it is that exists between us, it goes to the soul, far deeper than the surface chemistry you say to look beyond. I am a soul seeker. You are a soul seeker. And two kindred souls can make for a great passion, for it's in the soul where passion thrives. Maybe that's what is at work here."

He patted her hands and freed them. "But on to less serious matters," he said. "Let's talk about food. What are your favorite odd concoctions?"

"Odd concoctions?"

"Yes, like peanut butter on hot dogs, one of my favorites. Has to be melted peanut butter, however."

"Nope, you're not tempting me at all with that one. As a teenager I did enjoy dipping my French fries into my milkshake, if that counts," she said.

And on it went until they decided to drop the crazy concoction game, leave paradise, and go get a pizza. Over slices of sausage and pepperoni, he raised a second time the idea of her joining the sheriff's department. Once more she put off an answer, saying she would soon decide. She learned long ago that for her to drain the emotion out of a career decision, she would need to sit down and put pen to paper and list the positives and negatives of such a move. It was part of her decision-making style. Viewing it from the distance of the written word enabled her to consider the potential losses and gains in a strictly objective manner.

At day's end, in the comfort of her home, she was back to the personal, debating whether a moment's worth of passion is worth a month or more of heartache. She had been down this road before, the one where men will say anything to win your hand. "Yes, I'd love to have children...yes, I'll swear off the liquor...yes, I enjoy having your grandmother around," and so on. Alex Murin had yet to promise anything but an unbridled passion for her. It brought to bear the old adage if you want something bad enough, you'll likely get it.

Bothered, if not bewildered, she took to bed, her mind on the kiss still coursing through her body.

CHAPTER TWELVE

The trip home was uneventful for Adam. Truth be told, anything short of a mid-air collision would not have detracted from the excitement of his find. He had it in mind to call Tamra before his arrival in Tampa but the opportunity never presented itself in the rush of travel, so he decided to wait until the next morning when he could deliver the news in person.

Following a restless night punctuated with visions of people walking around in bathrobes, he headed off to work, prepared to rejoin the battle on his home turf. Playing catch-up at his desk prior to the formal opening of the workday, he jotted down a to-do list. First, make copies of the Murin letter to Alina. Second, verify Oleg's translation. Third, provide Mr. Quigley an update on the investigation. Fourth, check on the cultural exchange connection. Fifth, check passenger lists of incoming flights originating in Irkutsk, Russia.

His list completed, Adam plucked the Murin letter from his pocket and was headed for the copy machine when Tamra walked in, reminding him he'd left an item off the list---the briefing of his office manager.

"Well, hello, how was your vacation?" she asked. "I didn't expect you back this soon."

"I didn't expect me back this soon," he said. "Do you have time for a briefing?"

She shoved her purse into a desk drawer and smoothed her skirt. "Yes, sure."

Adam finished making the copies and stepped back to his desk. "Pull up a chair," he said.

"Why did you cut the trip short?" she asked.

Adam held up one of the copies. "Because of this."

Her eyes widened in expectation.

"It's a letter from Murin to his girlfriend," he said.

She stiffened. "How did you come across it?"

"A bit of thievery," he said. "But how we got hold of it doesn't matter. It's what's in it that counts."

Eyeing her as she eyed it, he handed over a copy.

She gave it a glance. "It's in Russian."

He smiled. "Oh, you want a translation," he said, trifling with her.

He pulled Oleg's translation from his back pocket.

"Okay, here goes…'My Dearest Alina, the path to our happiness is now open. She was easy to take care of. There is little else to say other than I look forward to seeing you soon. Love always, Alexei.'"

"When was it sent?" Tamra asked, adopting a matter-of-fact manner.

Her seeming indifference caught Adam's attention. "The envelope was postmarked March 8. Why?"

It was before Alex had met her, but that was small comfort at the moment for Tamra. She struggled to sort out the thoughts and images tugging her in opposite directions, neither of which led to a safe haven. She handed him back the letter. "Adam, there is something I must tell you."

"What is it?"

Her thoughts collected, she strove mightily to take the emotion out of them before delivery. "While you were away, Alex Murin and I have seen each other on a couple of occasions."

"Seen each other?" Adam asked, taken aback.

"He stopped by the office one day and asked me to join him for lunch, and I did. I thought no harm could come of it, believing I might even be able to gain further information on the case."

"And did you?" Adam asked smartly.

"Nothing, excepting it was his wife who was the cheesecake lover, so he said."

"Great. And the second get-together? What came of it?"

"He took me for a morning ride in the country."

"And since he wasn't the cheesecake addict, you went along." Adam's retort was sharp. "Look, Tamra, if this was anyone else but the guy who is the target of our investigation, I would have no problem. Your private life is your business, except when it interferes with our business, which is to serve our clients. It is not our business to become emotionally involved with suspects."

"If it makes any difference, there was no discussion of the case," she said.

"Did he ask about me? Where I was? What I was working on?"

"He asked where you were. I told him you were on vacation, but not where."

"He's a detective, Tamra, highly trained in this line of work...more so than I. The truth is by now there's a good possibility he knows I was in Russia, knows I was at the bar with you that night at Orologio's, knows it was you in his home helping the cleaning lady."

She attempted to cope with the deception rendered bare by the letter but recognized it was mostly of her own making.

"If you want me to resign, Adam, I will."

Adam sighed his discontent, not only at the suggestion, but the entire matter. "No, I don't want you to resign and here's why. I was the one who stuck your head out from the start, the one who gave you the assignments. I am as much to blame for this as you." Adam looked her directly in the eye. "Nevertheless, I need to know before we go any further: can I count on you with this case...with this job?"

She flinched from having to hear the question. "Yes, you can."

Adam noted the disappointment tinged with anger in her voice. "You expect him to call again?"

159

"Yes."

"How soon?"

"I can't be certain but you needn't worry which side I'm on, Adam."

"Time to get back to work then. I'm headed over to the International Cultural Exchange Center not far from here to see if there's a record of a Russian cultural exchange group having visited here within the last few years. We received info on our trip there was a mission from Irkutsk. It's important to establish if, when, and where there was a reconnection between Alina and Murin."

"Alina was part of the mission?" Tamra asked.

"Yes, and I need to find out if Murin hooked up with her during their stay. Also, I'd like for you to call a man by the name of Buddy Fears." Adam scratched down the number for her. "Tell him I referred you and that I need for him to check the passenger lists of incoming flights originating in Irkutsk in the next month for the name Alina Novikov."

"What about the Assistant District Attorney? Are you intending to notify him of your discovery?"

"Not at this stage. I still need to tie up some loose ends to bolster the case, particularly the reconnection matter."

"He called right after you left on your trip. I informed him you were on vacation. He asked if I could contact you. I told him it would be difficult because you were on the road and unavailable. I asked him if he wanted to leave a message and he said no."

Adam nodded his understanding. "Also, remind me when I get back to give Charlton Quigley a call to give him a status report."

"Adam?" she said as he rose to leave.

"Yes?"

"What you said concerning the possibility of Alex Murin knowing the details of our investigation. I understand where you are coming from in this regard and I also understand his wanting to learn what else we are up to. However, and I don't mean to make this all about me, but I---"

"What are you trying to say, Tamra?"

"I know I may be coming off as naïve in saying this, but it's me he also wants," she said with as little self-importance as she could muster.

Adam took the letter and scanned it once again, peered above it at his office manager, turned and left.

•••

The International Cultural Exchange Center was a one-office, one-desk, one-woman operation located in a small office complex adjacent to the downtown region. The middle-aged woman sitting behind the desk wore a white ruffled blouse with a navy blue dress. Her dark brown hair was swept tightly back in a bun. From her desk she flashed Adam an engaging smile on his arrival. "It's a good thing you came in now. We are open six months out of the year and close at the end of the month," she said by way of greeting.

He explained his reason for the visit, which prompted her to scoot her chair to the side in front of a desktop computer. "Let's see...you are looking for information on a Russian cultural exchange mission occurring sometime within the last two years. Correct?"

"Yes ma'am...from Irkutsk, Russia," he said.

"How do you spell it?"

"I-r-k-u-t-s-k."

In rapid-fire order, she punched in search commands and checked results, scrolling up and down to peruse the entries. "Here we go...yes, almost a year ago there was a group from Russia here."

"Do you personally recall them?"

"No, I came on board this year."

"Any photos or records of those who attended?"

She resumed searching through the entries. "I don't see any photos indicated...but hold on a second, there may still be something in the hard copy files. She proceeded to scoot her chair to a metal file cabinet positioned behind the desk. Picking through the folders, she paused to pluck one out and finger its contents. "This might interest you," she said. "It's a group photo of members of the mission."

She handed it to Adam who at once recognized the woman standing left of center in the photo. It was Alina Novikov, looking very much like the Ice Maiden he recalled from the Caviar Café.

Adam pointed to the photo. "These are the members alright," he said. "Do you have a list of local guests? I assume these groups conduct a seminar or host a reception of some sort."

"Yes. They normally put on a program open to the general public."

Adam looked about the office. "How do you squeeze them all in here?"

"We don't. We have a shared meeting room in the building. It holds over a hundred people."

"Are registrations required for these events?"

"We do not require registration. However, we do maintain guest lists."

"May I see those guest lists?" he asked politely.

"May I ask the purpose of your visit?"

"Yes, you may. I recently returned from a trip to Irkutsk, Russia, and learned while there, of the exchange mission to Tampa. I was interested in seeing who from here participated in the event."

"Are you looking for someone in particular?" she asked.

"Yes, a man by the name of Alex Murin."

The woman went into her chair scooting routine, spending a few minutes at the computer followed by a few at the file cabinet. Finished, she turned to Adam. "Sorry, but there is no Alex Murin listed."

"You're sure?" Adam asked.

She hesitated. "Well, there is another file cabinet in the back corner. However, I don't know if there is anything in it relating to this event, since the files date much further back than the files in this cabinet."

"Would you mind checking?"

"No, not at all."

The woman moved to a padded gray cubicle he assumed served as a storage area.

"Do you mind if I use your phone?" he called out to her. "I need to check in with my office."

"Help yourself. Dial nine first."

In a twisted way, the fact there was no Murin listed might perk Tamra up a bit, he concluded. No question it was a setback to the case. A guy murders his wife over memories of his childhood sweetheart? Not the best of motives, he would agree.

"Thought I'd check in. Anything new?" he asked his office manager.

"Nothing yet, but I'm expecting to hear back from Mr. Fears soon. How's it going on your end?" she asked, the deflated tone lingering in her voice.

Adam noticed the woman returning from the cubicle, shaking her head at him as she did so. "There's no Alex Murin entered in the guest list," he said to Tamra straight out.

"Adam?"

"Yes."

"Look under the name Dmitri or Mitya Karamazov, or Dmitri or Mitya Fyodorovich."

"Dmitri or Mitya Karamazov? Like the brother in the Brothers Karamazov?

"Yes. He's Alex Murin's alter ego. He thinks he's Dmitri in real life."

"Hold on," Adam said, thinking this was adding a whole new ingredient to the case.

"Please check under the name Dmitri or Mitya Karamazov, or Dmitri or Mitya Fyodorovich," he said to the woman.

She scooted to the computer and once more scanned the guest list, this time raising a finger midway through and nodding affirmatively. "Yes, there is a Dmitri Fyodorovich listed."

"Bless you my office manager," Adam said and hung up without waiting for a reaction.

"Can I obtain a copy of the list?" he asked.

"I don't see why not," she said, pushing the print button.

Adam browsed the printout and check-marked the Fyodorovich name."

"Thank you…and what is your name?"

"Sophia."

"Thank you, Sophia."

Adam next dropped by a translation service he had utilized in times past. The translator on hand confirmed via a phone call and fax to a Russian language expert that Oleg's translation was correct.

On his way back to the office, Adam decided on an early lunch at the Metro Retro Diner, a popular hangout for neighborhood residents and students in the university section of town. There was no mistaking the diner's throwback theme. Painted on the outside walls in garish fashion were mural-like images of the classic fifties cars, including a '57 Chevy and '58 T-bird. The gaudiness continued on the interior walls with renderings of James Dean, Sal Mineo, Marlon Brando, and Marilyn Monroe. The obligatory black and white checkerboard flooring, blood red vinyl booths, chrome trimming, juke box, and soda fountain section with bar stools completed the theme. All in all, he could do without the décor. What he could not do without were the fat, juicy, charbroiled hamburgers, skinny French fries, and thick milkshakes. They required of him several additional laps around the block each week, but the fare was worth the price in human toil.

Upon entering, a waitress decked out in a dark blue hoop skirt and fluffy yellow blouse led him to a booth as Buddy Holly serenaded them in the background. No sooner had Adam placed his order, he was joined in the booth by a tall, slender, tousled-hair man close to his age. The uninvited guest wore a rumpled plaid shirt, corduroy slacks, and a taut face several days removed from a shave. He took a menu from the waitress who had yet to leave the booth, leaned his head on the palm of his hand, probed his chin with thread-thin fingers like spider legs, and ordered steak and eggs. "Separate checks?" the waitress asked. "Yes," Adam responded with no hesitation. The woman gave a quick glance at both of them and swished her way back to the kitchen.

"Excuse me," Adam said. "Did you not see this booth was taken?"

"What's the matter, you don't want company?" the stranger said in a surly voice. "This side looked to be empty to me." The guy's beady brown eyes were locked onto Adam's. "No, I prefer privacy," he responded. "I understand in Europe this is permissible, but we're here, not there."

"Do you know what it means to have a wife and two kids, Fraley?"

So the guy knew who he was. That opened up all sorts of possibilities. "If you're asking if I'm married and have children, the answer is no, but I presume you already knew that."

Ricky Nelson replaced Buddy Holly in the background, as the waitress poured them water, again casting glances at each of them.

"I do have a wife and children, Fraley, who mean more to me than anything in the world." He raised his thumb and forefinger, separating them by a fraction. "I came this close to losing them…this close!" he said, his fingers quivering at the thought. He lowered his hand. "But they were saved by a friend. Do you know what a friend is, Fraley?"

"I believe I do," he answered, temporarily abandoning the idea of talking the guy out of his booth.

"It took a friend to save my wife and children from the mentally deranged man who was holding them hostage. That's what the media called him…mentally deranged. Do you know who the mentally deranged man was, Fraley?"

"No."

165

"It was me," he announced, pounding his chest with a fist. "I was the one holding my family hostage, threatening to kill them, until my newfound friend stepped in to save us all."

A swishing skirt turned their attention to the waitress approaching with their meals, the smiley on her cherub face replaced by a worrisome one.

Adam's appetite by this time had been placed on hold, but he dug in anyway. His booth mate, however, did not waver from the topic on the table. He has the internal dialogue going on in his head that makes him unpredictable or dangerous, Adam thought. No sense trying to talk sense to the guy. He was the reincarnation of Boris. Oleg's ploy to escape the rail station situation came to mind but he dismissed it immediately. He didn't have a train to catch nor was he going to run from the guy.

Adam continued to eat with the eagerness of a child nibbling on vegetables. Presently, he noted the stranger's thumbnail digging into his forefinger, drawing blood as his intensity level rose.

"Who's the friend who stepped in to help you?" Adam asked, already having a good idea of who it was.

"Do you know my reason for being here?" the intruder countered.

"As a matter of fact, I don't."

"I'm here to make sure you never bother my friend again," he said, gripping his fork and steak knife and hovering them over his food.

"How am I bothering him?"

"By doing what you're paid to do…snoop."

Adam was aware any verbal slip on his part likely would ignite the guy's fuse, agitated as he was. A second glance at the interloper's bleeding thumb, however, brought him to the realization the fuse was already lit.

Fats Domino blared from the jukebox, taking over from Ricky Nelson. And in the parking lot, a sheriff's car pulled in right outside the window. Two burly deputies exited the vehicle and strolled into the diner, taking two bar seats directly across from their booth. The guy may be nuts and totally focused on his mission but not crazy enough to ignore the presence of the law, Adam surmised. Now that the law was on hand, Adam bit into his food with his usual relish, waiting for the intruder to make his next move.

As Adam took a sip of his milkshake, he caught from the corner of his eye one of the deputies glancing over his shoulder at their booth, not at him but at the stranger. A nearly imperceptible nod from the deputy to the nut at once cleared everything up for Adam. The blowback had begun. The word had gone out from Murin. It was time for the troops to rally in his defense.

The stranger's role was over. He signaled for the waitress and dropped ten bucks on the table for her.

"Did you not care for the meal, sir?" she asked, seeing he had not taken a single bite of it.

"No, it's the company I don't care for," he said and stalked out, shoving the interior doors open on the way out like he had just cleaned out the saloon.

Adam finished his meal to the tune of Sam Cooke. He paid no heed to the two deputies who remained perched on their stools as he left.

•••

Back at the office, Adam related the incident to Tamra. "I'm going to take a trip to the library to see if I can dig up something on the hostage case," he said.

"No need for that," she said. "I already did some background checking of my own while you were gone.

She reached into her desk drawer and pulled out the article she had copied, handing it to her boss.

Adam skimmed it, not knowing what to make of her initiative. "Any word from Fears?" he asked.

"Not yet. He said he would get back to us before the end of the day."

"Good thinking on the Brothers Karamazov connection. I didn't know you were a Dostoevsky reader," Adam said. "I once took a criminal justice class where the instructor included the Brothers Karamazov in the supplemental reading list. Now I'm regretting not choosing to read it. Can you give me a thumbnail sketch of it, so maybe I can put things in context?"

"Thumbnail sketch?"

"Or summary...or brief synopsis," he quickly added.

"As you may know, Adam, summarizing a Russian novel in a few words is more difficult than writing it."

He slid a client chair from the front to the side of Tamra's desk and settled into it, folding his hands in his lap. "Still, it might give me some insight into what's going on in Murin's mind," he said with a coaxing smile.

Tamra set aside a box of supplies she was unloading, scooted her chair away from the desk, and clasped her hands around a knee. "Okay, I'll give it a try. In short, it's a morality tale...good versus evil, faith versus doubt, believers versus non-believers. It's the story of a father and his three sons. They are a very dysfunctional family mainly due to their conflicting philosophies of life and absolute positions they hold on politics and religion. The father is an out-and-out depraved hedonist. One of his sons, Alyosha, is kind and religiously devout. A second son, Ivan, is an intelligent, avowed atheist. The third son, Dmitri, is sensual and intemperate, depending on his state of mind at any given time.

"What sets everyone off is when the father and Dmitri start chasing after the same young woman, Grushenka. After a lot of turmoil and soul-searching over the situation by members of the family, the father ends up a murder victim. Of course, Dmitri is immediately suspected. Eventually, he is charged with the crime and convicted, though in the court of public opinion he is regarded as innocent---"

"Is he innocent?" Adam interrupted.

"Yes, and disgusted with the entire criminal justice process he had to endure, he plans an escape to America with

Grushenka to start a new life with her, though he vows to return to Russia one day. And that's how the book ends…with the planning, not the doing." Tamra paused and threw out her hands. "There you have it, minus a few hundred thousand words."

"Who did away with the father?"

Tamra shook her head. "Some guy whose name I forget."

"Why did he do it?"

"He was listening too much to Ivan Karamazov who convinced him good and evil are false concepts and people are free to do as they please without worrying about moral consequences."

"On the scale of dark and light sides, where does Dmitri fall?" Adam asked.

"Not in the middle…on one end or the other, though a professor might tell you differently," Tamra said.

"And the Tampa detective Dmitri---or Alex as we know him---where does he fall on the spectrum?"

"I don't know him that well, Adam," she said firmly. "I've only seen glimpses of one side of him."

He needn't ask which side that was.

"As for parallels," she continued. "The plan to escape to America with his lady friend is the most obvious one."

"I agree. Again, thanks for the connection. I didn't realize you were steeped in the classics."

She shrugged it off. "I wouldn't say steeped. I do my share of reading. In fact, the interior of our house resembles a library," she added.

"With wooden shelves, I hope."

"Of course," she said. "Wood and paper…you can't have one without the other."

Adam slid a client's chair from the front of her desk to the side and took a seat. "How long have you been collecting?"

She lifted her eyes in thought. "Counting the contributions of my grandmother, nearly fifty years. Some people purchase entire collections, others, like restaurants and decorators, purchase them by the box load for display purposes. We've built our collection one-by-one. I view them as timelines in my life. Music or scents trigger memories for many people. Books trigger memories in me."

"Your grandmother was the one who got you hooked on books?"

"Yes. She read to me as a child while babysitting me. I now read to her."

"Eyesight problem?"

"Yes. She suffers from a severe case of macular degeneration. Her great challenge is in the selection of books to read. Sometimes, she will get halfway through a novel before she realizes it's one she's previously read. On a couple of occasions she has waded through an entire one before the realization kicks in. Since I started reading to her, I've made it a point to avoid repetitions. Ironic, isn't it? Reading supposedly prolongs the memory, yet at the same time it can be an indicator of memory loss."

"How old is your grandmother?"

"We celebrated her eightieth birthday last week."

"Have you considered audio books?

"It's a sharing thing with us, Adam. Yes, we can listen together, but it's not in the family tradition. However, since we're running out of shelf space, we may have to go the audio option or else we'll be putting shelves in the bathroom and kitchen. When it comes to books, 'don't go near the water' is a good motto."

"How do you have them arranged? Subject? Author?"

"A very practical arrangement…by size," she said.

"I once knew a guy who arranged his personal collection by the color of their covers," Adam said. "He had them in the shape of a rainbow."

"Must have involved an interesting book selection process," she said.

"Do you and your grandmother share the same tastes in subjects?"

"My tastes are derived from hers. I alternate between the classics and recreational reading, mainly British mysteries. We've always enjoyed reading about faraway places. Oftentimes we would get out a world map and decide together what region we wanted to read about."

"Have you visited any of those faraway places?"

"Between here and Pennsylvania is as far away as I've been…one of the reasons for the books. If you can't see the world, why not bring it to you."

The phone buzzed, cutting into the conversation. Adam immediately reached over to lift the receiver from its cradle and return it. "I've heard it said a personal book collection reveals what you know, what you believe, and what you think," he said, picking up where they left off. "If someone were given the opportunity to browse your collection, what conclusions might they come to regarding you?"

She paused to contemplate. "Well, if you separate out my grandmother's contributions and considered mine solely, they'd probably conclude I'm not a 'now' person."

"Lots of history?"

"Historical fiction and classics in the main. The recreational reading I get from the library."

"Did you ever consider going into the bookstore business?" he asked.

"With the way the independents are going under? Not a wise move in this environment. Besides, bookstore owners who operate their business as a hobby rather than a profit-making exercise, as I likely would do, are destined to become another bad small business statistic. So, I've decided it's better to be a collector than a dealer. However, if I did open one, I'd want it to be in one of those old converted houses with lots of nooks and crannies to explore."

"What about rare books? Are you into them?"

"If we happen to come across one in a thrift store or garage sale, we will add it. We certainly don't go out of our way to collect them, since we are not dealers. Our object is to limit our holdings to what is of interest to us. Otherwise, we would be overflowing into the bathroom or kitchen."

"Book appraising…any interest there?"

"I don't have the qualifications or the interest."

"Do you do any writing of your own?" Adam asked, digging deeper into the personal.

"I kept a journal as a child, if you want to call that writing."

Tamra knew her boss was making nice to mask his disappointment in her. In truth, he had a right to be. The separation of the personal and the professional in the workplace was a difficult divide to honor on many levels. Moreover, she had turned a deaf ear to her own advice. Not only did she fail to look beyond the pretty face…worse yet, she did not look behind it in spite of the warning signs. Still, she was not alone in her misjudgments. Alex Murin was a detective in the sheriff's department. Didn't that count for something? Surely, the people who conducted the screening process for such a responsible position were no less culpable than she in passing judgment. As is, any thought she had in joining them was now put to rest. And yes, the letter was damning, but was it final in its meaning? Explanations were due all around, not the least of which was the one owed her by Alex Murin, or Alexei Murin, or Dimitri Karamazov, or Mitya Karamazov, or Dimitri Fyodorovich, or Mitya Fyodorovich, or whatever his name was at the moment."

"I understand a diary or a journal is a valuable resource for a writer in later life. It resurrects for them the thought process of a child." Adam said.

"Right now, I'm more concerned with the thought process of an adult," she replied.

"Have you ever considered continuing your formal education?" he asked.

"I have, but my grandmother needs my support…time-wise and money-wise."

"I could check with my advisor at the college. She may be able to steer you to some funding sources."

"If and when I get settled into this job, I may pursue it. Meanwhile, I'll have to travel the self-taught path, she said.

Which is pretty much what you're doing on this job thanks to my poor mentoring, he wanted to say.

Tamra resumed unpacking the office supplies. "You asked me to remind you to call Charlton Quigley," she said, dispatching him back to his desk.

He called Quigley, assuring him he was making definitive progress on the case and should have something for him within a week or two regarding the accuracy of the accident report.

By mid-afternoon he had caught up with the pile of work accumulated during his absence and decided to take a break...a stroll around the block to bask in the warm Florida sunshine his body had been deprived of while away. If he had had the time, he would have hopped on over to Al Lang Field to take in a Cardinals' spring training game, sit in the bleachers with a hot dog and beer, and gaze out over Tampa Bay between innings in an atmosphere as far removed from the rigors of Siberia as could be. Instead, he settled for the pleasant fragrance of blooming frangipani mingling with the salt air flowing in off the gulf as a gentle reminder he was indeed back home.

Upon his return Tamra greeted him with the news Fears called.

"And?"

"Alina Novikov will be arriving on Air France flight 754 at eleven thirty tomorrow morning."

"Oh yeah? To think I could have missed her by extending the trip an additional day," he said, recalling the suitcase he tripped over in Alina's bedroom. "I'd better get on the phone to the Assistant D. A. to bring him up to date."

He reached Rusty Daniels in his office and briefed him on what had transpired since they last talked. Daniels made no comment, except to say he would join Adam at the airport in the morning to greet the Russian visitor.

How satisfying will that be? Adam mused, picturing Novikov's face when she sees him there to greet her. There was another greeter he could count on being there in addition to the Assistant District Attorney. No way was Alex Murin going to miss picking up his trophy.

CHAPTER THIRTEEN

A half hour prior to Alina Novikov's arrival, Adam settled into an airport waiting room chair, which offered from a cautious distance an unobstructed view of the Air France arrival gate. Somewhat perplexing, neither the Assistant District Attorney nor Alex Murin was in sight. He checked the monitor mounted above the waiting area. Flight 754 was on time.

Thirty minutes later Flight 754 was taxiing toward the arrival gate at the same time Daniels was stepping briskly from the main terminal aisle to join him at the rope line.

"I don't see Murin around," Adam said.

Daniels glanced about but kept mum.

The first strings of disembarking passengers drifted out of the terminal, trailed by the arriving flight's main body of travelers. Among the latter was the Ice Maiden, outfitted in a striking white sundress, striding gracefully in their direction.

"Is this her coming?" Daniels asked.

"Yes," Adam said, prompting Daniels to pull from inside his suit jacket a large piece of folded paper, which he at once unfolded and held out to her. Printed across it in large block lettering was the name Rusty Daniels.

Puzzled by the makeshift sign Daniels put on display, Adam shifted his attention back to Alina who glanced at him with her usual bland countenance before turning to the Assistant District Attorney.

"Hello Mr. Daniels," she said, as if they were longtime professional acquaintances.

"Hello Alina," Daniels replied in like manner. "This here is Adam Fraley. I believe you two have met."

175

She acknowledged Adam's presence with an expressionless nod.

Adam wasted no time in jumping in on the conversation. "Wait a minute...do you two know each other?" he asked, dumbfounded at the development.

Daniels ignored the question. "I've reserved through Airport Security a small conference room down the hallway where we can sort things out in private," he said, "Follow me."

Oh yes, this needs sorting out, thought Adam. What the hell was going on? What have I missed? How could these two know each other? If they do, then why the sign? And where in the hell is Murin?

They marched in silence to a metallic gray conference room where a stocky, middle-aged man in a sheriff's department uniform occupied one of six chairs encircling a table.

"Alina...Mr. Fraley...this is Sheriff George Cartwright. He's agreed to join us," Daniels said by way of introduction.

Adam took a seat at the table with the others and waited for the explanations to flow.

Daniels clasped his hands in front of him and cast a glance at Adam. "First, I would say to Mr. Fraley this is a case of both good and bad timing. A week or so ago, I received a long distance---a very long distance---call from this woman. It concerned Detective Alex Murin. It so happened Alina knew Murin from her childhood days. To put it simply, they were sweethearts. Over time they became separated when Murin's family moved away from Irkutsk, their hometown. In the long period since, they had no contact with each other until this past year when Alina traveled to Tampa as part of a cultural exchange mission. Somehow, Murin got wind of it, probably from an article that appeared in the local paper announcing the event. It featured a group photo of the mission members, including Alina here, a photo Mr. Fraley informed me yesterday he also had uncovered at the cultural exchange center..."

"Thanks for letting me in on your discovery of it, following my discovery of it," Adam mumbled sarcastically to himself.

Daniels paused. "At this point, I am going to let Alina pick up the story."

Alina's expression had not varied a smidgen since her appearance at the arrival gate. She was all business as usual. "As Mr. Daniels explained, Alexei Murin showed up at our cultural exchange event," she said in her Oleg Popov quality English. "I had not seen him in a very long time and was both surprised and pleased when he appeared. We had a day off from the conference and he asked me to accompany him on a tour of the region. I agreed, since I was anxious to view as much of Florida as I could on the trip." She paused to catch her breath, the first sign of a crack in her icy demeanor. "It turned out to be a terrible mistake."

Further cracks in her comportment appeared as she continued. "He was not the same fellow I remembered from my childhood." She shook her head, as if to shake away the memories. "He took me to a remote area and suddenly became very aggressive in his manner and opinion, telling me he had waited all his life for me to return to him, wanting me to make love to him right then and there. Fortunately for me, there was a crew of men in uniform working the area. "It prevented him from going any further in his advances."

"We believe it was a crew from the Florida Fish and Wildlife Service working the area," Daniels interjected.

Recovering her composure, Alina continued. "At my insistence, he drove me back to the cultural center. After I returned home to Irkutsk, I started receiving these letters from him telling me how unhappy he was...that he was married to a woman he did not love. He said someday he would be rid of her and then I could move to America to be his wife. I did not reply to any of his letters. His last ones, however, greatly concerned me. In particular, the very last one indicating to me he may have done away with her by violence, since he did not mention divorcing her. That's when I contacted Mr. Daniels."

"This occurred at nearly the exact time you left for Russia, Mr. Fraley. I informed Alina of what happened to his wife and asked her if she would be willing to come here as soon as possible at our expense and swear in an affidavit what she told me over the phone, and if she could bring along the letters. She said she would. However, she could not bring the important last letter because it had disappeared from her home." Daniels paused, then added, "I will tell you this is one brave lady."

He angled his head to look at Adam sitting next to him. "Did you by chance break into her house and take the letter?" he asked, clearly confident of the answer to come.

"Yes, I did," Adam stated directly. "You mean to tell me she was planning on bringing you the same letter I lifted?"

"Yes, Fraley. You brought back the letter she intended to carry on her person. She set it atop her dresser as a reminder to not forget it. She already had packed the other letters in her luggage and they are in our hands. If it's any satisfaction, you beat her back."

A wry smile formed on Daniels' face. "She could easily charge you with home invasion and burglary but has thoughtfully decided not to press the matter and turn it into an international incident. She is grateful the letter showed up in our hands."

Alina raised her hand to make a point. "Based on my recent experience with him, I feel Alexei Murin craves intimacy. He cannot live without it. Otherwise he becomes very intense. I worried what happened to me could happen to another person, perhaps something even worse."

Adam recalled his stay in Irkutsk in light of the revelations. The stoic image of Alina, in particular, as she waited on them at the Café Caviar was viewed in an entirely new light. To realize she knew at the time she was about to take an exhausting emergency trip to the States to assist in a case that unbeknownst to her involved the men she was serving dinner to was as incongruous as he and Oleg's unawareness of it. In the end, did this mean his trip was a wasted one? With Alina on board and the incriminating letter in hand, Daniels would have had his case. Still, the answer was no. He could not believe the

Assistant District Attorney would have pursued the matter without the impetus he and Tamra provided it from the beginning. No, without the pressure he was feeling at home, Daniels might have blown away Alina's long-distance concerns. Besides, how could he consider the trip a waste? He got the taste of Russian life he'd always longed for, not to mention the friendship of Oleg.

"Now, there is more to the story," Daniels continued. "Murin did have charge of an unmarked sheriff's car the night of the accident, though we can't place it at the exact scene. Nonetheless, we examined it again and discovered miniscule particles of the infamous pumpkin cheesecake pie on the floor of the vehicle. We also reviewed the autopsy report and the examiner stated it was possible for someone to have bashed Vickie Murin's head into the steering wheel two or three times in the same exact spot on the forehead, which could induce death. And there's one other matter I'm going to let Sheriff Cartwright explain."

Adam was still attempting to absorb the flow of new developments when Cartwright began. "The rural locale Murin drove Alina to, is known as 'The Veiled Lagoon.' Several years ago a young woman went missing in this area. The only lead we had was one given to us by an old farmer driving down the rural road leading to the lagoon on the same day the woman was reported missing by her parents. He said he passed a dark colored van traveling in the opposite direction with a man and young woman in it matching the missing girl's description. He did not get a good look at the man driving. His attention was drawn to the woman who appeared to be arguing with the way she was flailing her arms about. The farmer dismissed it as a lover's quarrel. The case went unsolved. There was never any evidence of foul play uncovered. It was determined early on she was likely a runaway, given she was always at odds with her parents."

"Are you saying Murin had something to do with her disappearance?" Adam asked impatiently.

"Maybe not her disappearance, but he had something to do with the case," the sheriff said. "The young woman who went missing was a waitress at Orologio's. Her name was Marly Madison. Murin requested to be the lead investigator, saying she was a favorite of the deputies who hung out there. He was given the assignment. Murin also owned a dark van at the time."

"Did anyone think of putting two and two together?" Adam asked in frustration.

"He was above suspicion," the sheriff meekly replied. "We now are reopening the case."

Adam threw open his hands. "With all due respect, I have to ask. How in the hell did he make it to detective in the first place? Wait, let me rephrase that. How did he make it into your outfit in the first place?"

His question visibly unsettled the sheriff. "To be honest, we dropped the ball big time. His record in the States was clean. The problem was the background check carried out or not carried out by officials in what was then the Soviet Union. They informed us he had a degree in police work from a university in Omsk. At our request they sent us a copy of the certificate of degree, which appeared to be in order. We attempted to get further information on him but the Soviets were highly suspicious of American law enforcement inquiries at the time. All we got was the line 'there is no record of illegal activity on the part of the subject.' Unfortunately, we gave him the benefit of the doubt. This past week we checked again with Russian authorities and happened to get the right guy on the line this time around. He did some checking and it turns out Murin for a period operated under assumed names. This was after he graduated." The sheriff sifted through his notes. "The fake names were Anton Borzov and Yuri Lebedev. Borzov, in particular, had a shady background. He was charged on two occasions with sexual assault and battery but was cleared on both accounts due to lack of evidence. There were no witnesses willing to come forth and testify against him. Once he was cleared, he changed his name back to Alexei Murin and skipped the country."

"He didn't move to America. The guy fled to America," Adam said in response. "Is there sufficient evidence to charge him in his wife's death?" he asked.

"There is now, plus he's on the run, which is strong evidence itself."

"On the run to where?" Adam asked in earnest.

"He disappeared as of this morning," Daniels said. "It's likely someone tipped him off."

Adam's heart leaped to his throat. "But you have no idea who tipped him or where he's headed?"

"He could be headed for Cuba, the Caribbean, Russian communities up north, or Irkutsk. We don't know. However, now that the scales have fallen from our eyes, we can get busy tracking him down."

Adam turned to the stoic figure of Alina. "He did not know you were coming today?"

"No."

Unless he was checking passenger lists himself, Adam thought. "I have to get back to my office," he said. "Did you receive the copy of the Murin letter I faxed you?"

Daniels patted his folder. "Yes. We'll be in touch if we need anything further."

Adam nodded his appreciation to Alina and left, concealing his anxiety in the casualness of his gait out the door.

CHAPTER FOURTEEN

At first, curiosity got the best of Tamra, delaying her lunch plans. She was marking time till Adam returned with his account of Alina Novekov's arrival. It stood to reason law enforcement officials would take their time thereby ensuing everyone's rights were honored in the legal process lest missteps cost them in the end. A better option, she decided, was a quick trip to the deli and back prior to his returning.

She grabbed her purse, exited the office, and trotted to her car, oblivious to the figure stepping out from behind a parking lot signboard to follow close on her heels. Reaching for the car door handle, she felt the grip of a hand on her wrist. "Alex, you startled me," she exclaimed as she recoiled from the contact.

"I need a ride," he said.

"Where's your car?"

"It's out of commission,"

"Where do you need a ride to? I have to get back to work shortly."

"Come on, I'll show you."

The grip on her wrist tightened. It could be an errand of some sort or another trip to Orologio's, she convinced herself. "Okay, but we'll have to make it fast," she said.

He loosened his hold and she let him in. Igniting the engine, she proceeded to drive to the parking lot exit where she pulled to a stop. "Now where?" she asked.

"To The Veiled Lagoon," he said.

"Alex, I have to get back to work. I'm…"

He gripped her wrist again. "Tamra, do what I say."

She slowly released her foot from the brake and eased out into traffic, realizing her mistake. To make matters worse, she caught a whiff of alcohol on his breath.

"I miss my wife terribly, you know," he said, gazing out the passenger window.

"I'm sure you do," she said, attempting to humor him.

"She was uncomplicated...plain but uncomplicated...not like most women. She didn't get under your skin like you sure as hell do. And never did she consider betraying me."

Murin shifted his attention from out the window to her in anticipation of a response.

"You're not thinking I betrayed you?" she said.

"That night at Orologio's with your boss perched on a stool next to you, pretending he's just another guy looking for some action...Remember? You don't think I'm that stupid, do you?"

She had no reply.

"Well...do you?"

"No."

"Or his taking off for Russia. I suppose you didn't know what he was up to?'

"I work for the business. I'm expected to carry out my duties."

Murin let out a guffaw. "How perfect, just like the good German doing what's told her. Well, we Russians know all about good Germans doing their duty."

"That's nonsense, Alex," she said in irritation. "Remember? I'm the woman with the Russian name."

"Okay, a collaborator is what you are, joining with the enemy to rid the world of all the bad guys, or taking all the fun out of life, as Dmitri would say."

"If you recall, Alex, Dmitri found redemption at the end," she said, in an appeal to his understanding.

"But I'm not at my end, Tamra. I'm still enjoying the sinful middle," he said, as they entered the on ramp to the interstate.

•••

Adam arrived to an empty office. The lunch hour had passed. Worry welled up inside him, overwhelming all other worries. Where was she? He could not recall a time when she left the office without informing him. He searched for messages but came up empty. He called her grandmother who said she should be at work. Out of reasonable explanations, he sat down at his desk to contemplate the unthinkable. Did she tip Murin off? Run off with him? No, to the second question, not with a loving grandmother at home who was dependent on her.

The buzz of the phone sent Adam's forefinger flying to the lit button. "Hello?"

"Mr. Fraley...Daniels here. Wanted to let you know we uncovered how Murin got wind we were on his tail. Seems he hacked into our computer system and accessed a message detailing our scheduled meeting with Alina Novikov."

"Any news on his whereabouts?"

"None. I'll let you know as soon as we find out something."

"Thanks," he said, grateful Tamra was not likely the tipster.

He was back to believing she was on an errand or possibly an extended lunch, something simple to explain her absence, in other words back to his wishful thinking.

•••

"Oh, and did I tell you I'm a huge pumpkin cheesecake lover?"

"I thought that was your wife who was."

He chuckled. "I lied, but I certainly wasn't lying about how terrific you looked at lunch that day...not so terrific though in my home with the wig and dopey uniform."

She didn't buy his knowing of the home invasion, or else he would have checked carefully at the time for missing items including the pie pan. No, he must have figured it out later when he noticed it missing.

"Now you're back to your sexy self, so all's right in our little corner of the world...right?"

She felt the clasp of his hand above her knee.

185

"Get you hand off my leg, Alex," she snapped.

"You know, the one thing better than pumpkin cheesecake pie is the feel of hose on a woman's leg, especially yours."

She swatted at his hand without success.

"What happened to all the love between us," he quipped, before removing his hand. "Has that boss of yours made a pass at you yet?"

She shook her head.

"Not a bad looking guy, I have to admit. Looks like he keeps himself in shape."

He slumped back into his seat. "Do you sense the tension rising in this car?" he asked. "I think you'd better be more concerned with the fuel situation. We're nearly out," she said.

Murin leaned over to check the gauge. "Just like a woman to drive on an empty tank."

"I wasn't expecting to take this trip," she said.

"There's a station at the turnoff to the lagoon up ahead. Pull in there."

A short distance further, she took the exit and turned into the station lot, nearly empty of cars.

"Pull up to the last pump," he directed.

Like the good German, she followed his order.

"I'll do the pumping and, like the gentleman I am, I'll also do the paying," he said.

Murin slipped his hand inside his jacket and pulled out not a credit card but a handgun. He rested it between his legs. "This is a Beretta, Tamra, in case you didn't know. The point to be made is I have nothing to lose, which, according to law enforcement officials, makes me armed and dangerous. In saying that, they would be wrong on only one count. I have nothing to lose but you. He slipped the pistol back inside his jacket and leaned across the seat to snatch the keys from the ignition. He then reached into his back pocket to retrieve a pair of handcuffs, slapping one of the cuffs around her wrist and the other around the steering wheel. "This is to make sure you behave yourself...for now."

Murin hopped from the car and set about gassing up the tank. Little did he know that not only was she lax in keeping the gas tank full, she also was remiss in keeping the car clear of clutter, which is why she never got around to removing Adam's toy from the backseat floorboard where she had stashed it till she could find the time to take it to her nephew.

She stretched her free arm through the small opening between the door and the driver's seat, snatched the bag containing the phone and dragged it over the backrest and into her lap. Instantly, she took her purse and stuffed it atop the mobile phone.

Murin cracked the door open in a flash. "What are you doing?"

She gave him a perplexed look. "Looking for some tissues. What did you think I was doing...reaching for a gun?"

Murin returned to the pump, jammed the nozzle into the tank and pulled the trigger.

Tamra peeked at her tormentor who had his back to her. At once, she resumed shuffling through the bag with her free hand, locating the phone and lifting it out above the bag where she was able to view the numbered keys. She was unsure whether it even had a battery, Carefully, she raised the receiver, propped it between her ear and shoulder and dialed 911. As luck would have it, all she received in return was static. She repositioned the unit a bit but the static continued uninterrupted. Her heart sank. Quickly regaining her composure, she took another peek at Murin and made a second attempt at dialing.

•••

Adam considered calling the Assistant D. A. to alert him his office manager was missing and could be with Murin willingly or unwillingly. However, he was uncertain whether it would complicate the search effort or not, so he...

The phone buzzed. In the same instant his finger hit the lit button. "Hello?"

Static cracked over the line.

"Hello? Hello?"

He strained to hear a voice.

"…Adam?" he heard through the scratching.

"Tamra, is that you?" he called out. "Where are you?"

More static. Through it came a faint response…The Veiled Lagoon, and the line went dead. He slammed the phone down. "Where the hell is The Veiled Lagoon!" he shouted to the office walls. He hurriedly dialed Rusty Daniels, whose secretary answered. "I need to speak to Mr. Daniels immediately."

"Mr. Daniels is on a conference call. May I take a message?"

"This is important…very important," Adam said.

"Sir, I'm afraid he is unavailable at the moment," she said.

"Well then, I do have a message for you and him. Listen carefully. I don't care if he is on a conference call with the Pope. If he is not on this line within thirty seconds, I'm going to personally come over to your office and wrap that phone cord around both your necks."

•••

Tamra returned the handbag to the rear floorboard, unsure of her effort.

Murin finished filling the tank, jumped back into the car and freed her wrist. "Miss me?" he said.

She took her time traversing the familiar path, dodging torn tree limbs tossed onto the road by an overnight storm. She was of a mind to hit one or simply run her car into a tree and take her chances but thoughts of her grandmother going it alone dissuaded her.

"Driving one-handed on this road is not exactly a smart move," he said. "What's that you're holding in your other hand?"

"Nothing."

"What do you mean nothing? What is it?"

"It's a medal my grandmother gave me."

"Oh, yeah? What kind of a medal?"

"A St. Christopher medal."

"How quaint, an accident prevention measure from medieval times…no wonder you're driving with all deliberate speed," Murin said. "Say, wasn't he the guy who got demoted?"

She gave no answer.

"Religion and sex. It's a good mix, you know. More than a few times we caught kids---even adults---breaking into churches to have sex. They'd do it right on the altar, if they could…right in His face." Murin laughed. "It was the only incentive for them to go. They liked the high." He turned to her. "Why do you suppose that is?" he asked.

"I have no idea," she said.

"Oh, come on Tamra, sure you do. To get the ultimate sensation, you have to sacrifice what's most sacred to you and embrace the forbidden. Oh, yes, you see in me the forbidden fruit…or to put it in street terms…the very bad boy. Well, the bad boy's here and ready to do service."

From his other jacket pocket, Murin withdrew a near empty bottle of vodka and gurgled down the remaining portion. Lowering the window, he hurled the canister backhand into the underbrush. "Soul seekers…kindred souls…two of a kind," he scoffed, casting a sidelong glance at her. "You were buying into that drivel, weren't you? The truth is, Tamra, you're soulless. That nice body of yours, or the temple as your favorite brother Alyshoa Karamazov might call it, is all you got, though I have to admit it's enough to make a guy forget Alina."

Tamra held her tongue. Why stoke his anger further? Anything she had to say would be greeted with further contempt. She no longer was a person but an object of scorn whose sole purpose was to satisfy his cravings.

"Are you aware Dostoevsky spent four years in an Omsk prison?" he asked. "I attended school in Omsk. I learned it was in prison he came to realize one must go through the degradations of life to experience the goodness of it. In other words, experience the extremes to avoid being stuck in the worthless middle." Murin turned to her. "You've yet to experience the degradations of life. Have you yet, Tamra?"

She remained silent, drawing a contemptuous glare from her tormentor. "Well, have you?"

"I plan on skipping that step," she replied.

"I want you to know I will feel terrible after all this is over with," he said. "It's how the cycle goes. I'm like the guy who confesses a sin knowing full well he will commit it again. Does that make any sense...me being sorry for what I'm about to do?"

Her mind raced back to a safety seminar sponsored by a professional women's group she attended not long ago. "The surest way to avoid physical assault is to not place yourself in the company of male strangers while alone," a former state prosecutor said.

She imaged in her mind Murin sitting next to her, refusing to look his way. How stupid of her to place herself in this situation, she thought, and then thought again...no...no...no...not how stupid of her...how unmanly of him. Coming into view were the stands of trees forming the outer wall of the lagoon.

"Park it in the same spot as before," he commanded. "We'll make everything as before, except for the ending...or the non-climax, I should say." He gave out a mocking laugh and reached across to pat her on the thigh. "You won't be needing this car anymore."

She eased the vehicle to a stop. If only she could ease herself in the same manner...stop her life and start it again when the bad parts---the degradations---had passed.

Murin seized her by the wrist and dragged her across the front seat and out the door.

"Hold it," he said, taking his jacket and handgun and tossing them into the car's front seat. "I won't have need for these."

With Tamra in tow, he led her through woods darkened by a low-hanging, overcast sky and into the clearing cradling the lagoon. He took her to the knoll, releasing her wrist before plopping himself onto the matted turf. He patted the surface next to him. "Come on, have a seat."

Under Murin's watchful eye, Tamra slipped off her shoes, smoothed her skirt, and swept her hair to the back, tying it in a small knot...

"There you go, get comfortable."

...before bolting for the water.

The lagoon stretched long and thin, maybe thirty yards wide at the point she entered it. If she could beat him to the far side, her car awaited with the keys in the ignition and the gun in the front seat.

She splashed her way across, through one, two, three feet of cool water, the commotion spooking flocks of gray and white herons to flight. Behind her, she heard Murin flailing in the water in feverish pursuit.

Midway across, the water rose above her waist, tempting her to break into a swim where she might gain an advantage. But the water level abated as she drew nearer the far shore, so she continued with her slog, resisting the urge to glance over her shoulder for fear of slowing her crossing.

The approach of the shore energized her. She was now knee deep in the water and prepared to break into a run when she felt the clamp of a hand around her ankle.

Murin twisted her on her back and attempted to grab hold of her free ankle. A swift kick in the face, however, caused him to lose his grip and she was, at the moment, free again. Even so, she was cut off from the shore, the specter of Murin staring her down from four feet away.

"Give it up, Tamra," he calmly stated.

If spoiling for a fight, she would give him one. "I'd never surrender it to you," she said in defiance. "You're far from the redeemed Dmitri. You're the animal Dmitri following in the footsteps of his depraved father...a chip off the old block."

She once more slogged her way back across the lagoon despite the sapping of her strength. This time the clamp around her ankle came early on in her crossing and she was unable to wrest free.

In a trice Murin had her by both wrists, dragging her on her back to the shore and up the incline to the grassy bed. "Come on, Tamra...up to the altar we go."

Overhead, a cawing crow rode a gust of wind from the pending storm, cocking an eye to the scene below, a lone witness to the transformation of an Eden into one of Dante's pits.

Her last ounce of effort was gone. She'd always known if this time ever came, she would have to disembody herself, deny her attacker the first instant of gratification.

She looked past the shoulder of the man-animal groping her to a place far away, first and last to her, and none other.

"Look at me!" Murin shouted. "Look at me!"

Her mind was elsewhere, as were her eyes, their intensity of focus causing her attacker in frustration to glance behind him, in time to see the two-by-four sized tree limb a foot from his forehead.

The thud echoed across the clearing, the blow sending Murin into wobbly world.

"Get off her, you bastard," Adam shouted.

Murin rolled onto his side, as Tamra scrambled free.

The Russian tried to right himself on shaky legs, but a shove from Adam to the chest landed him on his backside.

Setting aside his weapon, Adam grabbed Murin by the ankles and dragged him halfway down the incline, positioning his head against the slope. He picked up the limb, measured it against the cut on his forehead, and hammered him a second time on the identical spot, the blow splitting the piece of wood, sending half of it flying like the business end of a cracked bat. He tossed away the stub in his hand and scoured the area for another limb.

"Adam...stop!" Tamra yelled.

He found another limb, this one bigger and sturdier. So what if they sent him to an anger management class. He could sit through the entire course relishing this moment.

"Adam...please stop! You'll kill him! Please!" she screamed.

He stood over the fallen detective and watched the red rivulets course down his face and onto the ground. He bent to check his pulse, noting he still had one. He then tossed aside the limb, his fury spent. Slowly, he walked to the water's edge. A crack of thunder signaled the arrival of the storm. Presently, droplets of rain began their pitter-patter at one end of the lagoon and spread rapidly across the entire channel, giving it the appearance of boiling water. Boiling water without the boil, Adam pondered in the pouring rain.

He walked back up the incline and planted himself on the soggy turf. Through the murk and sodden veils, he sighted a column of vehicles with flashers on coming down the road in silent procession.

He turned to Tamra who had her face to the gushing rain. "You okay?'

She nodded.

Bereft of thought he joined her in putting his face to the downpour.

CHAPTER FIFTEEN

A two-story, whitewashed red brick house fronting a rusted red brick street was testament to the historical charm represented by South Tampa's burgeoning home restoration movement. As a construction foreman, George Madison and his wife Diane, an interior decorator, had clearly taken advantage of the challenge presented them. The result was a structure as rich and textured on the exterior as it was on the interior. Such was the craftsmanship on display that Adam could easily envision the couple building a cabin from scratch on the shores of Lake Baikel, the differing elements notwithstanding.

At the Madison's invitation, Adam took a seat on an orange armchair, one of the many brightly hued living room furnishings bathing in light from the morning rays streaming through sheer cotton curtained windows. Accent rugs featuring vivid graphics rested on oak wood floors, adding to the lightened look. To Adam the restoration appeared total and complete. The only thing missing was a daughter.

George Madison sat beside his wife on a yellow couch opposite from Adam. He was a man of medium build with closely cropped dark hair, drawn face, a dense stubble on his chin, and the deep tan of a man who spent most of his waking hours outdoors. Both he and his wife were reserved in manner, as quiet as the sunbeams stealing into the room. Any cheerfulness they may have once possessed had long since been drained from them. "The District Attorney's Office called us right before you called to let us know about Detective Murin's arrest," Mr. Madison said.

"Yes, the office informed me they had contacted you," Adam said. "They had no objection to my visit as long as you had none."

"Needless to say, we were surprised," Mrs. Madison said, stroking a lock of her shoulder length light brown hair. "Mr. Daniels said they were unsure if it had anything to do with Marly's disappearance. What do you think?"

"I'm not sure either, though it's certainly an interesting turn of events," Adam replied.

"If you're not sure, why are you here?" Mr. Madison asked.

"It's because we are unsure," Adam answered. "There's a sense of unfinished business regarding the Murin arrest and it has to do with your missing daughter. In all your dealings with him, was there anything you found unusual?"

Mr. Madison slowly shook his head. "Nothing at all. He seemed sincere throughout in his effort to find Marly," he said. "He kept us informed all along as to the steps they were taking. It is difficult to believe he was somehow involved in her disappearance. If so, it is very discouraging to say the least."

"Do you recall Marly bringing up Murin's name at any time prior to her disappearance?" Adam asked.

The two glanced at each other and shook their heads no.

"Did she ever mention a place called 'The Veiled Lagoon'?" Adam asked.

"We'd never heard of it until this morning when Mr. Daniels referred to it over the phone," Mrs. Madison said.

"Has Murin confessed to anything regarding Marly?" her husband asked.

"Not to my knowledge," Adam said, convinced Murin was not likely to do so.

"It is so frustrating," Mrs. Madison said. "At first, everyone suspected she was a runaway but we were certain that was not the case. Yes, she was a bit rebellious at times but there was no real reason for her to run from home. We knew something terrible had occurred."

"We've come to the point where we're just looking for closure," her husband soberly said, as if reconciled to her fate. "We don't want it to turn into a cold case, though it appears to have become one."

Adam noticed through a window a young woman tending to a garden at the rear of the house. "Did Marly have any siblings?" he asked.

Mrs. Madison looked to a series of time lapsed family photos lining the living room wall. "She has a younger sister, Carly."

"Is that her in the garden?" Adam asked, motioning toward the window.

Mrs. Madison leaned forward to glimpse out the opening. "Yes, that's her."

"Would you mind if I spoke with her briefly?" he asked.

She looked to her husband. Obviously, they did not want to subject their remaining daughter to further trauma if at all possible. "Please make it brief, Mr. Fraley," Mr. Madison said. "She's already gone through enough grief."

"I will," Adam said and left, conscious of how quickly a happy home could be turned into a hollow one by the stroke of a cruel hand.

"Are those desert roses?" Adam asked on approaching from behind the strawberry blond kneeling in the dirt, pruning shears in hand.

"Yes…are you another investigator?" she inquired in return, as though they all came in the same size, shape, and color and she needn't look to see.

"Yes, I am. My name is Adam Fraley."

She snipped several limbs from one of the desert roses. "What is it you'd like to know?" she asked, continuing with her pruning.

"You were away at college the day she disappeared?"

"Yes."

"Did you speak with her often while you were away?"

"Yes."

"Did she have a boyfriend?"

Carly hesitated and took a deep breath.

"Sorry for the probing," Adam said. "It's the necessary evil of our profession."

"Between school and work, she had no time for boyfriends."

"Did Carly enjoy the outdoors?"

"She loved the outdoors. When she could squeeze in the time, she would either be hiking trails, riding horses, or paddling kayaks."

"Did she ever mention a place called The Veiled Lagoon?"

"Not to me."

"I know this may seem irrelevant but can you tell me what your sister's field of study was in college?"

"She majored in psychology and minored in history, though she switched her minor later on."

"To what?"

"Russian literature."

"Did she give a reason for the switch?"

"She had been reading some of the Russian classics and decided the subject was more to her liking. The course was taught in English, so there was no language problem."

"Did she mention what classics?"

"No."

"Did you speak with Alex Murin during the course of the investigation?"

"He interviewed me once. All I could tell him was that I was certain my sister was not a runaway."

"Did your sister know of him prior to her disappearance?"

"Yes."

"Did she speak of him?"

"My sister was a year ahead of me in college. She was in her last year at the community college here while I was in my junior year at Florida Gulf Stream University over on the east coast.

On one occasion a couple of my classmates came home with me to spend the weekend in Tampa. That Friday evening we went to Orologio's. My sister was working behind the bar. She introduced us to Murin and a few of his buddies from the sheriff's department who were hanging out there."

"That was the extent of it?" Adam asked.

"Yes."

"Nothing of note occurred between him and your sister during the evening?"

Carly paused in her pruning. "I don't know if you would consider it noteworthy but I did notice him engaging in a favorite male pastime at happy hours."

"What sort of pastime?"

"Like I said, my sister was working the bar. At one point she was mixing drinks and had her back to us. I noticed Murin giving her an extra amount of attention."

"Fixated on her?"

"No, not fixated on her. Fixated on body parts. It's what men do…nothing noteworthy about it."

Carly resumed her pruning, moving to a gardenia bush, keeping her back to him. Her attention to the plants reminded Adam of efforts by prison officials over the years to introduce gardening as a therapeutic step in the rehabilitation of prisoners. People who make things grow demonstrate an appreciation for life and are less prone to violent behavior so the argument went. Of course, whenever the subject was broached someone would invariably point to a serial killer who at one time was a master gardener. True, there were always the exceptions to the rules, yet it was the exceptions that kept him in business.

"You have a nice garden here, Carly," Adam said, trying not to sound condescending.

A teardrop landed at the base of the bush she was working on and melted into the soil. A second followed.

"It's not my garden. It's Marly's," she said. "I'm just tending to it while she's gone. We're waiting for her to come home, Mr.

Fraley. I'll say to you what I said to Mr. Murin...just find her and bring her home."

CHAPTER SIXTEEN

He never would understand the ways of women. "Are you sure you're up for this?" he asked.

"Yes. It's something I need to do," Tamra said from the front passenger seat of his pickup.

Adam pulled his truck to within ten feet of the outer rim of woods guarding the lagoon. "Beautiful morning," he said.

"Yes, it is," she said, grabbing a towel from her lap and bounding from the vehicle. "You stay here. I didn't bring a suit."

"Yes, ma'am."

He watched her disappear into the woods. Left to himself, he set his mind adrift on the tropical breezes sweeping across the surrounding landscape.

A few minutes later, from the lagoon's cocoon, he heard a splash of water followed by the rhythmic lapping of a swimmer in motion, followed in turn by brief pauses…he assumed for her to catch her breath. The sequences were repeated, until broken by one long interlude, which led Adam to speculate on her condition. He listened intently for a sound to ease his mind, but all he could hear was the wind whispering through the long strands of Spanish moss, as if straining to tell him a story from across a mystical divide. Concentrate as he might on the airy voice, the message escaped him. Suddenly, the whistle of an osprey pierced the moment, calling Adam's attention to a bald eagle lifting from the treetops, a fish in its clutches, following a raid on its smaller cousin's nest.

Disquieted, Adam exited the truck. He walked to the passenger side of the vehicle and leaned against its side, his eyes never leaving the woods and the strands of moss gently swaying to the breeze. He closed his eyes and drifted into a meditative state, again concentrating on the call of the wind.

"Hi," she said, startling him from his reverie.

She stood before him, combing her hair while Adam gathered his senses.

"How was the water?" he asked in relief at seeing her.

"Reinvigorating…restoring…rehabilitating…rejuvenating… all the re's you can think of," she said, ending her combing and turning to face him.

He held her gaze.

"Thank you for coming along," she said, adding a smile, the kind to wash away the worry from the consummate worrier.

"From now on I'm putting you in charge of the deadbeat dad cases," he said.

She smiled once more. This one telling him he had much to learn about women.

They climbed into the pickup and Adam quickly had the truck off the clearing and on the road to the interstate. A half-mile along it, he came upon an intersecting road in the same rutted condition as the one they were traversing. He slowed the pickup to a stop and turned to Tamra. "Would you mind if we took a little side trip?" She shrugged her shoulders. "You indulged me. I certainly can indulge you."

Adam swung the pickup onto the intersecting road and headed north along a stretch of flatland marked by crisscrossing wooden fences sagging in their midsections from the ravages of age and weather. "We're going abandoned cemetery hunting," he said.

Tamra tossed him a bemused look. "Okay," she said.

"I got a call from my old boss last night. He was curious about the Murin case. Apparently, it made the news down in the Keys."

"Can't wean himself from the business, can he?" she said.

"Pete's not unlike the retired railroad guy or military vet. Once the occupation gets into your blood, you are invariably drawn back to it, so you start hanging around train yards or VFW halls---"

"Or crime scenes," Tamra interjected.

"More like trade shows or private eye seminars," Adam said.

"Why do I think this phone call from your former boss has something to do with abandoned cemeteries?"

Adam steered the rollicking pickup around a stump in the pathway, kicking up a cloud of dust and chasing a flock of crows feeding on a raccoon carcass at the side of the road.

"My boss said he once conducted a family history search at the urging of his wife who grew up in this area. It bounced him from place to place, one of which was an abandoned cemetery somewhere along this road.

"Are we looking to finish his business?" she asked.

"We're looking to finish unfinished business but not for him," Adam replied.

"There!" Tamra exclaimed, pointing ahead to an area of thick underbrush off to the side of the road. "See the markers sticking up?" she asked.

"Yes, I see them," he said, at once easing the vehicle to the side of the road adjacent to the graveyard.

Adam estimated the burial grounds covered an area of twenty-five square yards, most of it concealed by the heavy underbrush and thickset vines intertwining the wooden, concrete, and marble markers standing at every odd angle.

The two stepped gingerly through the shrubs and past the markers, noting names and dates on those visible through the brush. Inscriptions on a number of the markers were completely obliterated by the erosion of time. A few others, relatively new, were swept clean of pine needles and had withered flowers contained in mason jars and tin cans placed at their base.

Tamra turned to him with hands on hips, halting their procession through the rows of markers. "Adam, can you tell me what you are in search of, so I have some idea of what to look for?" she asked.

"Okay, I'll tell you," he said, overcoming his reluctance. "We had a conference at the airport called by the Assistant D. A. following the arrival of Alina. The Deputy Sheriff sat in on it. When it came his turn to speak he told us of the case of a young woman who went missing in this area several years ago. Her name was Marly Madison. Its relevance is that Alex Murin, at his own request, was named the lead investigator in the case. Marly was a waitress at Orologio's. Murin claimed she was a friend of his. The only lead in the case was provided by a farm worker who said he saw a young couple in a van he passed on the road to The Veiled Lagoon on the day of her disappearance. They appeared to be arguing. The farm worker only got a good look at the woman who matched the description of Marly. Murin, at the time, owned a van of the same color. Anyway, the case went unsolved and Marly was deemed a runaway."

"Murin was never suspected?" Tamra asked.

"No, he was above suspicion, according to the Sheriff. The fact is, without a body, the case for murder is a difficult one to prove."

Tamra appeared taken aback by the revelation. She turned her attention back to the rows of markers. "Her name is not going to appear on any of these," she said.

"No, it is not, but it's worth a look, since we were out this way. When I was talking to my old boss, he suggested it, saying he heard of it happening…killers burying their prey in an isolated cemetery, figuring it was not a likely place to be searched. One other point he made. Killers like Murin often will leave some kind of calling card to satisfy their ego, even if they make an attempt to conceal their deed…like it was a work of art requiring a signature."

Adam took a deep breath of the briny breeze blowing in off the gulf, shaded his eyes, and looked to the horizon. "There has to be an owner or caretaker of this land," he said.

His eyes landed on a lone farmhouse sitting in the middle of the flatland a mile or so down the road. "Let's go see if anyone in that farmhouse can shed some light," he said.

It was a vintage, white, two-story clapboard farmhouse bleached gray by the merciless Florida sun. Fronting it was a large live oak with a thick trunk and long horizontal branches that served as rods for the long strands of moss hanging from it. Beneath the swaying strands rested a small pond blanketed by hyacinths. Located at the side of the farmhouse was a small pen where two mottled horses stood with their heads over the fence, as if drawn by the sight of the visitors. Adjacent to the pen was a tool shed in front of which sat an elderly man in a wicker chair filing down the blade of an axe.

Adam parked his pickup on a gravel drive that circled the front of the property. Their appearance prompted the man to set aside the axe and shuffle his way toward them.

He was dressed in railroad overalls, under which he wore a stained, caramel-colored t-shirt. He had a tanned, whiskered face and stringy brown hair flowing from under a weather beaten baseball cap.

Adam leaned his head out of the truck window to greet him. "Yes sir, can I ask you a question?"

The old fellow gently tipped his cap. "Go right ahead."

"Do you know anything about the cemetery down the road from here?   It looks to be abandoned for the most part."

"It sits on my property, so I know it like the back of my hand," he said in a gravelly voice. "And you're right in calling it abandoned. The county says I have to maintain it, since it's on my property, and if I don't, they will do the upkeep and bill me. Well, I'm in no position to maintain it and they ain't done the upkeep. So there she lies…as dead as what lies beneath her."

"Would it be an inconvenience for you to give us a quick tour of it? We're researching a missing family member and would like to make sure we are covering all our bases."

"Don't see why not. It's been a while since I've taken a walkthrough of the place myself."

Adam was aware it was less his cajoling than the sight of Tamra in the front seat that spurred the old man to his decision. She scooted over, as the fellow circled the pickup like a giddy teenager. "Hi," he said, climbing into the cab next to her. "My name is Gandy."

The trek back to the cemetery gave Gandy the chance to air his travails. He related how his property was once a thriving peanut farm, how the conglomerates came along to gobble up the small family farms, how he had no family to carry on the operation, how the big guys lured away all his help with higher wages, how he decided to shut down the operation and make do with what he had saved from the productive years, and, finally, how he had come to realize the only option left was to sell the land as the tax burdens were eating big time into his nest egg.

Back at the graveyard, Gandy stood amid the markers beneath a bright sun, removed his cap, wiped his brow with the back of his hand and asked the same question Tamra earlier put to Adam. "Can you tell me what you're searching for, so I know what to look for?"

"Do you recall the case of a young woman who went missing in these parts a few years ago? Adam asked.

Gandy's eyes narrowed, drifting into the past. "Yeah, I do, now that you mention it. Two sheriff's men came knocking on my door one day. Funny thing is, I thought they were here about the cemetery. But, nope, they were looking for information on a missing girl and wanted to know if I'd seen or heard anything. Told them I hadn't."

Two red wing blackbirds landed on a nearby marker and pranced and chirped at each other for a minute, drawing the attention of the three onlookers before taking to flight again.

"Do you recall anything else they said?" Adam asked.

"I remember them asking if they could take a look around the property. Help yourself, I said."

"Did they search the cemetery?"

"Don't know. They didn't mention it."

"By chance, do you recall the names of the investigators?"

Gandy chuckled. "No way. I do remember the guy who was doing all the talking had an accent and it wasn't a southern one...more the foreign type."

Adam directed Gandy's attention to where they stood. "Well, is there anything unusual you see here, something out of the ordinary maybe?" he asked with a sweep of his hand.

"Now that you've given me an idea of what you're after, let's take a look around," he said, motioning them to follow him. "Be sure to walk slowly to give the snakes time to get out of your way."

Adam cast a glance at Tamra. "Definitely don't want to disturb the snakes, do we?"

Gandy led them through the dense underbrush, past the gravesites, pausing here and there to yank aside branches or vine to expose the inscriptions.

"Wait a minute. This grave is missing its marker," he said, pointing to the mound of earth to his side.

Tamra stepped up to his side. "Did it have a marker?" she asked. "There are others here that don't."

"Yes, I know. I've dubbed those the tombs of the unknown. But this one did have a marker," he said, stretching his head back and forth to scan the immediate area. "Hold on here a minute. I'll be right back."

Gandy trudged down the road, brushing aside the shrubs and vines at a quickened pace, not giving the snakes much time to get out of the way, Adam observed. Finally, he stopped and called to them. "Found it...come take a look."

The two walked to where the old man stood holding back an armful of shrub to expose the missing marker. "Someone moved it from that grave to this grave. Must have been some kids playing around."

Tamra and Adam set their eyes on the inscription.

**IVAN
F. K.**

"It's a wooden marker, so they were able to scratch out the last name, the birth and death dates, probably with some pine needles, and add in the initials," Gandy said.

"Do you recall the man's last name?' Tamra asked.

"Sure do. It was Lukin. Ivan Lukin. When I first saw this marker, it grabbed my attention, because I once had a friend whose last name was Lukin. This marker belongs back up at the other grave." Gandy gazed down at the mound. "I'm not sure who's buried here."

Adam turned to Tamra who knelt at the grave, brushing away with her hand the twigs and pine needles covering it. "He couldn't resist, could he?" he said to her.

She shook her head no. "The rational Karamazov brother, the one who cleared the way to murder," she said.

"Not sure what you folks are referring to," Gandy said. "You know who's buried here?   "Marly Madison, the missing girl, is buried here," Adam said.

"How do you know that?" he asked.

"The murderer left his calling card."

"Are you sure it's the missing girl beneath here?" Gandy asked.

"Ninety-five percent sure," Adam replied. "The sheriff's department undoubtedly will be getting in touch with you to make arrangements for exhuming the body. I know you would like to switch the marker back to its proper place, but I suggest you leave it be for the time being."

"Sure," he said, releasing the armful of brush.

Gandy peered down at Tamra who continued with the cleaning of the grave from her kneeling position. "Ma'am is this Marly Madison related to you?" he asked.

Tamra averted her eyes from the two onlookers. "Yes," she said. "Closely related."

They drove Gandy back to the farmhouse, thanked him for his help, and set out for the long ride home.

CHAPTER SEVENTEEN

"Did you speak with Mr. Quigley this morning?" Tamra asked.

Adam stood at the foot of her desk, shuffling through the mail. "I did," he said. "I gave him a full report, though he had read the account in the morning paper. He seemed pleased."

"Wait till he receives the bill," she said.

"Winning will take the sting out of it," he replied. "It's the ultimate balm. Plus, I told him it came in a little higher than expected. I also reminded him that because of his willingness to step forward, Marly Madison and Vickie Murin, not to mention you, are all on track to receive justice."

The body exhumed was identified as Marly Madison. The District Attorney already had charged Murin with first degree murder, kidnapping, and sexual assault, according to the paper. Additional charges relating to Marly were now pending and her body was returned to her family for proper burial. Murin was scheduled for his first court appearance as soon as he recovered from lacerations to the head and a concussion.

"There's a package for you that came with the morning mail," she said. "It came from the Ukraine."

She opened her bottom desk drawer, drew out the package, and set it before him. Adam opened it, formed a big smile, and raised high one of the items contained in it.

"A can of mosquito spray?" she said.

"Inside joke," he said.

"Can you send such things in international packages?" she asked.

"Don't know, but it got here."

209

"He withdrew the other item, a large family photo of Oleg, his wife, and daughters, drawing another smile from Adam.

He placed the items back into the package, set it aside, and took a seat directly across from his office manager. "What's on your mind," he asked, his empathy rising to the fore.

She appeared back to normal but that was a surface observation at best. He needed something more, something to tell him everything was okay, that she had forgiven him for littering the ground around them with mistakes.

"At the moment, my mind is on my job," she said, "and that you wanted me to remind you of your appointment this afternoon with your academic advisor...your special friend," she said, the hint of a smile in her eyes, if not on her lips.

He would have to make do with it.

•••

"Your guide turned out fine then?" Nancy Egan asked.

"The best," Adam said.

"Glad to hear. I'll keep him in mind if another request comes up."

"He's giving up the job to return home to the Ukraine," he informed her.

"Oh...too bad. I'll pass the word along to Fred Jenkins."

"How are you and Professor Finley getting along," he dared to ask.

"Fine," she said. "We're planning a trip to Europe this summer...a ride on the Trans-Siberian not included."

The news she had taken up with one of his former professors did not unnerve him at the time. Their relationship was over and Martin Finley, as far as he could tell, was a man of good character.

"On an unrelated note," she continued, "Julie Hamilton averaged twenty-five points a game and led us to the regional championship game, which we lost by a single point, in case you didn't hear. I'm sure you're pleased with her play."

"As pleased as you," he said, noting the sarcasm in her voice. "I assume a compromise of some kind was reached?"

"More like a capitulation. Her father, her coach, and, sad for me to say, her professor came to her defense."

"Why doesn't that surprise me?" he said. "Longing for your old job yet?"

"No, the battle here is just getting started."

A silence settled between them. "Something on your mind?" she asked.

Adam gazed at her for a moment. "I nearly killed a man."

"So you were telling me."

"Managers are paid not to lose their cool. I lost mine big time."

"But you didn't kill him."

"That's what my former boss said."

"You talked it over with him?"

"Yes."

"And what did he say, if you don't mind me asking."

"He said it was too bad the bat broke."

"My turn to ask...why does that not surprise me?" she said, holding back a smile while closing a notebook on her desk. "Anyway, congratulations to you on completing your course work. The question now becomes...what are you planning to do with your degrees?"

"The same thing I'm currently doing," he said.

"You're not here today to seek my advice on the matter?" she asked.

"Yes and no," he answered. "No, I'm not seeking career advice today. Yes, I'm asking if you will continue to be my advisor."

She tilted her head, inviting further explanation.

"What occurred between us," Adam said, "I don't want to lose...I'm not sure how to put it...the core of it."

She leaned forward in her chair and interlaced her fingers on the desk. "I understand," she said. "Countless couples discover over the course of time they are friends foremost, which in the long run may be a far better thing."

"In the long run I may be settled in another part of the country, which means I'd have to make a point of not missing those wonderful class reunions," he said, his wry face on display.

"In that case, beware. As a former colleague of mine long ago said: 'the mind is like a freezer. The memories it holds, especially the pleasant ones, become perishable when exposed to their birthplaces.'"

He nodded his agreement and stood to leave. "Adam," she said, halting him on his way to the door. He turned to see her giving him one of those knowing smiles he had become accustomed to. "Someday, the right young woman will come along in your life. I'm convinced of it. And listening between the lines of your earlier story leads me to believe she may already have arrived."

ABOUT THE AUTHOR

Henry Hoffman is a former public library director and newspaper editor whose fiction and non-fiction works have appeared in a variety of literary and trade publications. He is the author of four previous novels, including *Bridge to Oblivion*, the first of the Adam Fraley mystery/detective series, which received the Florida Publishers Association's Gold Medal Award for Florida Fiction. He is a resident of Southwest Florida.